Spring in Stickleback Hollow

The Mysteries of Stickleback Hollow

By C.S. Woolley

A Mightier Than the Sword UK Publication

©2021

For

Jon David Beets

The villains in this story are named for him after he backed my cover overhaul Kickstarter. None of the beautiful covers on these books would be possible without him (or any of the other backers, but he funded the majority of them!)

Author's Note

Thanks for taking the time to read *Spring in Stickleback Hollow*, I hope you liked the book. As the series is becoming more established, my aim is to keep the books coming until the story of Lady Sarah is complete. For some, I know you will join us for a short part of the journey, for others you will be there to the end. No matter how long you join us for these Mysteries in Stickleback Hollow, it is wonderful to have you along for the ride.

Spring is a great time of year; a time of renewal and a time when we can reflect on the past so that we can move forward with our lives. These last few years, it has been hard for many people to see past the restriction and lockdown dates. My wedding has been delayed and it is still uncertain whether my family and friends will be allowed to travel by November, but as we go into 2022, I go in with the hope that Spring affords the wonderful and good surprises that life can have in store for us.

Though times are hard and uncertain, we can still find glimmers of hope. Stay positive in attitude and reach out to someone if you need to talk. There are a number of free services out there if you are struggling and need advice or just an ear to bend so you can unburden how overwhelmed you feel.

Please do not suffer alone, the world is not your burden to carry.

Kia Kaha.

The Characters

Lady Sarah Montgomery Baird Watson-Wentworth

The heroine

Brigadier George Webb-Kneelingroach

Lord of Grangeback and Lady Sarah's Guardian

Bosworth

The butler

Mrs Bosworth

The housekeeper

Cooky

The cook

Mr Alexander Hunter

A huntsman and groundskeeper of Grangeback

Pattinson

An Akita, Alexander's hunting dog

Constable Arwyn Evans

Policeman in Stickleback Hollow

Doctor Jack Hales

The doctor in Stickleback Hollow

Miss Angela Baker

Seamstress and mother of the Baker boys

Stanley Baker

Son of Miss Baker

Lee Baker

Son of Miss Baker

Reverend Percy Butterfield

The vicar in Stickleback Hollow

Mr Thomas Egerton

Son of Wilbraham & Elizabeth

Mr Edward Christopher Egerton

Son of Wilbraham & Elizabeth

Mr Richard Hales

Son of Doctor Hales

Mr Gordon Hales

Son of Doctor Hales

Miss Jessica Hales

Sister of Doctor Hales

Derwyn Evans

A welsh gentleman, brother of Arwyn, son of Edryd

Miss DeVille

A young woman of Stickleback Hollow

Mr Oliver Henry Brown

An American Gentleman, Cousin to the Egerton Family

Sylvia

Lady Sarah's Companion and Lady's Maid.

Edryd Evans

A welsh gentleman, farmer and father of Arwyn and Derwyn

Bronwyn Evans

Wife of Edryd, mother of Arwyn and Derwyn

Lady Szonja, Countess of Huntingdon

Cousin of the Egertons, Ally of Lady Sarah

Lady de Mandeville

Lady Sarah's Nemesis

J. D Beets

A Villain

T. J. Land

Another Villain

Chapter 1

Life is a chaotic mix of joys and disappointments.

At least that was what Edryd Evans had found to be true.

He had experienced many of both, and for the moment, the joys far outweighed the disappointments, but he still had many years ahead of him for that to change. He sat in his high backed chair before the fireplace in the old Welsh farmhouse.

His wife, Bronwyn had long since retired to bed, but he had too many things on his mind to languish between the sheets so early in the day.

A letter had arrived that morning from his son in Stickleback Hollow and contained the most disturbing news. He had read the letter twice and found that even then the events that had occurred over Christmas seemed too fantastic to be real. Yet, he had spent many weeks living in that manor, and he knew how easily Lady Sarah found trouble. A lot of what he had seen and heard during his time at Grangeback he had kept to himself, at least until his son Derwyn came home. He knew without corroboration, Bronwyn would think the farmer was teasing her.

But the grave news contained within the letter had pushed out all thought of anything other than the predicament that lay before him. He now knew he had lost one of his trusted farm hands to murder and that it had been due to the knowledge he carried. He could not change the fact that he had sent a man to his death, or that he had been the one to invite such trouble into his household, but he could protect those still under his care from further unnecessary risk.

He sighed and closed his eyes. The smell of the fire, petering out in the grate before him, filled his nostrils with a scent that brought him great comfort. The smell was mixed with the glass of whisky that sat to the left of his chair. It was not something that many of the other farmers drank, but he had always had a taste for the richer things in life.

He thought about his father, a man of strong, but down-to-earth beliefs. A man who called those who drank anything more than beer "too fancy for their own good". Edryd wondered what his father would have done if he had found himself in such a position. He laughed to himself as he realised that his father would never have found himself in such a predicament and would have had one or two strong words to share with Edryd if he could have seen his son now.

There was nothing he could do to stop danger from coming to his door now. He had invited it willingly by involving himself in the life of his estranged son. He knew that his wife would never forgive him if he backed away from all of this now and that he would be something of a laughing stock in his own household. His wife had married a young, brave man, not afraid of his father, not afraid to do things differently and strive for a better life for all those around him. To stand up to his father, only to run away from murderers and kidnappers would be the height of cowardice as far as Bronwyn was concerned.

The men who worked for him on the farm would similarly lose their respect for him. He sighed a second time, much deeper and heavier than before.

He was glad that his daughter was gone and married. She at least would be safe. There was no reason for anyone to involve her or connect her to the household now, though a niggling fear that Bronwyn might have written to her about the affair gnawed at the back of his mind, he managed to temporarily quiet it with the idea that perhaps the letter would have gone astray.

The clock in the hallway chimed the hour.

Edryd picked up the glass of whisky and drained it.

He would not show any form of weakness. His sons had stood firm despite the danger, and he could not do any less than that.

He read through the letter once more before he tossed it into the fire. The dying flames licked around the edges of the paper, slowly consuming it until it was nothing more than spots of ash in a pile of many others.

He stood up and stretched, but it was not his bed he was bound for. He walked to his study and pulled out some parchment and a pen. He wrote quickly but made sure that his message could still be read.

Arwyn,

Come at once.

Bring all those that are involved.

We may have found what you have been searching for.

>   *Edryd*

It was short but to the point. He would not risk any further details in this letter. Should anyone intercept it, they would have no frame of reference or guide to what it might be. He was certain that it would be enough to bring all of those from Stickleback Hollow he had left behind such a short time before, and he was more than certain that danger would follow with them.

He stood and made his way outside. The cool night air was a welcome blast across this face, a reminder of the place he called home, and a refreshing tug at the pride he felt to be born a Welshman.

Across the farmyard was a barn that had been converted into rooms for the hands that worked on the farm but did not have homes of their own. It was never locked as the men were often going in and out of it at all hours, especially during the lambing and calving seasons.

But for the moment it was quiet and still. No animals were born in the cold of winter, but spring was coming and it would soon be a busy time for everyone.

He walked past two doors down the corridor and knocked on the third one he came to. There was no answer.

He knocked a second time, harder than before, and heard two men inside stirring in their sleep.

He slowly turned the handle of the door and walked into the door, careful to close the door behind him again.

"Wake up, you lazy good for nothings," Edryd hissed and snatched the blankets from on top of two sleeping men.

The room was quite spartan in design, with two beds against opposite walls, two trunks at the foot of each bed to store belongings in, two small tables beside each bed for personal items and a washstand in the middle of them. Chamber pots were stored under the bed as it was often too cold to make the trip to the outdoor bathroom in the cold of the winter night. To the right of the door was a small stove with a kettle. The stove heated the room and the kettle provided the essential cups of tea that could rouse any man from the doldrums of aftersleep.

"What time is it?" one of the men groaned.

"It's the wee hours, but I need you both, now. I'll put on the kettle," Edryd said and the two men slowly sat up and reached for their blankets, that Edryd had unceremoniously dropped on the floor.

The kettle was already full, a practice the men had gotten into the habit of doing - fill the kettle before bed and there would be no need to go outside in a nightshirt, and it did not take long to boil. Each man had his own enamel mug next to his bed, and a shelf above the store held the tea leaves. The milk was normally brought straight from the cows by Bronwyn after the dawn milking, but the cows would not be ready for milking for several hours now, so the tea would be black.

Despite the lack of milk, each man greedily accepted their hot mug and drank the liquid with gratitude.

"What do you need us to do?" the second man asked after his third gulp of tea.

"I need you to go to Cheshire. This letter is to go to my son. Don't stop on the road for anyone. Keep riding until you get there. If he is not at the police house, go to Grangeback Manor and give this to Lady Sarah," Edryd said seriously.

"What's in it for us?" the first man asked.

"You'll get your year's wage each for doing this one job, and whatever gratitude my son or Lady Sarah are willing to bestow upon you," Edryd said firmly.

"It's a simple job for such a large reward," the second man frowned.

"It's simple, no doubt about it, but it is also dangerous. If you stop on the road, if you are diverted, you'll not make it back to spend your fortune," Edryd sighed.

The two men both stopped drinking their tea and looked at one another for a moment. The silence stretched on and forced Edryd to ask,

"Will you do it?"

"Yes." the two men replied.

Chapter 2

Grangeback Manor was strangely silent. The lull between Christmas and Spring always meant that there were fewer visitors at the great country house, but this was not the reason for the quiet.

The Baker Boys were in the village, cleaning out their mother's shop and making sure that the mice had not eaten too much of her fabric.

There was tense anticipation in the air. It had been months since Miss Baker had left on the business of the Crown, and she had not been alone. The Lord of Grangeback, Brigadier George Webb-Kneelingroach had been with her as well as the Chief Constable, the Countess of Huntingdon, and Mr Henry Cartwright.

And the group was due to return any day now. Every member of the household staff at the manor was hard at work, cleaning every inch of the household, which left Lady Sarah with time on her hands.

The day-to-day running of the estate had not been placed on her shoulders. The staff knew their duties and could carry on happily with only major decisions being made by Lady Sarah as and when they needed them.

There was far more that the brigadier would have taken care of in normal circumstances, but with his sudden departure, it had left very little time to explain everything that running the Grangeback Estate entailed.

Doctor Hales had taken up residence in the great house to assist Bosworth, the Butler, and Mrs Bosworth, the housekeeper, with the tasks that could not wait for the brigadier's return.

But as far as Lady Sarah was concerned, the doctor had moved into the house to keep her company and act as her guardian, and help to take care of the Baker boys.

The doctor was in the village attending to the poor souls who were suffering from a bout of influenza, and looking forward to moving back into his home.

The only guest visiting the manor was Derwyn Evans, and he had gone to the lakes for a few days with his fiancée, Miss DeVille.

So Lady Sarah was alone, and rather than getting

underfoot in the house whilst the servants cleaned in a fury, had chosen to take her horse, Black Guy, to explore the grounds. She enjoyed riding out in the cold air and seeing signs of spring breaking through the lingering winter snows.

She had chosen to ride on the far side of the grounds that lay away from the village and rolled into the surrounding farmland.

Today, she did not wish to be found or have her thoughts interrupted by anyone else.

At breakfast, she had received a letter from the Russian Ambassador, Carlo Pozzo di Borgo, that had consumed her thoughts throughout the meal and into her riding time.

The letter had been a pleasant one, it carried no warnings of danger or threats of terrible things to come. Instead, it was a letter that declared abiding friendship between the pair and informed the young lady that no matter what might happen, she would always have a staunch friend and ally to call upon.

It was a strange letter to receive, and filled with politeness and sincerity in equal measure. It was astounding to Lady Sarah that English was not the Corsican born ambassador's first language.

She had rarely received letters in her life. Those that she had been sent tended to be more direct and to the point than the ambassador's letter.

Her mother had often received piles of letters from friends of hers living in every corner of the globe. The young lady had often found it strange that her mother had so many people to write to and that so many people wrote back.

Now Lady Sarah was convinced that the letters were less social and had more to do with the business that her parents conducted on behalf of Lady de Mandeville.

She wondered how her perception of her parents could have been so wrong. She had always thought they were such upstanding people before they died, so much so that she would never have believed they worked for a woman like Lady de Mandeville or that they would be murdered.

It certainly has been an interesting few years, she thought.

She let her thoughts swirl around inside her head as

she and Black Guy roamed across the farthest corners of the grounds, stopping for a small picnic at lunchtime under the protection of a line of oak trees. Black Guy pawed through the last vestiges of snow to find the best blades of new grass to munch on.

The days were still short, so it was mid-afternoon when the light began to bleed from the sky and sent the lady and her faithful steed back to the house. It would be too dark to see properly by 6 o'clock even though the sun would not fully set for another half an hour after that. The heavy cloud cover that threaten fresh spring rains stole the weak light from the sky, so Lady Sarah was always sure to be back at the manor at 5 o'clock.

The letter from the Russian Ambassador still filled her thoughts as she untacked and rubbed down Black Guy. It was the grooms' responsibility to take care of all the horses, but it was a point of pride for the young lady that she looked after her horse when she had finished riding him.

She made sure there was plenty of hay in his manger and the water in the stone trough was not frozen. He would be fed in another hour by the grooms when all the horses ate, by which time, Lady Sarah would be safely ensconced in her library.

Rather than take the shortcut from the stables through the kitchens, Lady Sarah made her way around to the far side of the house where her rose garden stood. There was a small door that led into a back passageway in the great house, which allowed the lady to come and go with a minimal amount of fuss and it also meant she did not disturb the busy household staff.

She used the side stair to return to her room, bathe and dress for dinner, before descending to her library. It had become a simple routine over the last few weeks and it was a routine that had, so far, kept the lady out of curious mysteries and the trouble they bought.

But as she opened the door to the library, all thoughts of her routine and the Russian Ambassador were chased from her mind.

"I'm sorry to arrive unannounced, your ladyship," Constable Arwyn Evans said stiffly. He was stood in the middle of the library and flanked by two exhausted-looking men.

"What is it, constable?" the young lady frowned and

looked cautiously at the two men.

"My father sent these men to me, they carried the message that Mr Kvietkus was entrusted with," Arwyn said, trying to calm any suspicions the noblewoman had.

"And what is the message?" Sarah asked, her heart was pounding in her chest with anticipation.

"They believe they have found them. We should go to my father as soon as possible," Arwyn said firmly.

"We?" Lady Sarah frowned.

"All of those involved, even those we wish to leave behind," Arwyn smiled at her sadly.

"Then we shall go as soon as your friends have rested. I will have Mrs Bosworth make up rooms for them. I would also suggest that you remain at the Manor tonight. After last time, it would be best to prevent anyone from travelling alone at night," Lady Sarah replied, trying desperately to keep her excitement in check.

"We're going to Wales!" Stanley Baker cried from inside the wall of the library and a moment later, one of the panels on the wall swung open and the twins bounded out of it.

"What have I said about eavesdropping on my

conversations?" Lady Sarah asked with mock irritation.

"We weren't trying to eavesdrop, we were just making sure that you were safe," Lee protested.

"Well, in that case, go fetch Mrs Bosworth, and tell Cooky there will be another three joining us for dinner," Lady Sarah sighed and gave both boys a reassuring smile.

Chapter 3

The walls of the lodge seemed much closer than they ever had before. Mr Alexander Hunter had returned to find his home packed away, awaiting his arrival. Everything had been stored with such care, and the furniture was covered to prevent it from gathering cobwebs and dust.

As a man well over six feet tall, he often found that most buildings were too small for him, and the lodge was no exception, but it had been his childhood home and had never seemed too small to him before now. The biggest difference was that he had spent more time at Grangeback in the last few months and his tour of the northern country had made his residence seem far smaller than it ever had before. Even without the presence of his dog in the house, it felt as though he could not stay inside for more than a few hours. He had even spent some nights sleeping out in the forest. It had been cold, but he had built small fires and a shelter that had kept out most of the cold, but it felt much better to be outside than to be inside the lodge.

He had avoided Grangeback for the first few weeks that he had been back. He knew that he had made the biggest mistake of his life when he abandoned Lady Sarah and left Stickleback Hollow without a word of warning. He had broken his engagement and left her to cope with the grief of losing their child alone, as well as dealing with the pressures of Christmas at the Manor. Her life had been in danger too, and he had not been there to protect her. Instead, it had fallen to one of the few men that Mr Hunter respected, Wilbraham Egerton, military officer and confirmed bachelor.

Wilbraham had been badly wounded protecting Lady Sarah, and when Alex had heard the news, he felt even more guilty about leaving. But he could not change the past now, he could only try to move forwards as best he could. Lady Sarah had forgiven him for all that he had done to her, but she had refused to marry him. He should have known better than to expect her to fall back into his arms and act as if nothing had happened, but there was another man who was now vying for her affection.

An American cousin of the Egertons, Mr Oliver

Henry Brown, was visiting Cheshire, and upon meeting Lady Sarah had discovered a reason to stay.

He was a charming man with his own wealth, and a good prospect for any young woman that might catch his eye, but Mr Hunter knew how special Lady Sarah was. He had lost her once, but he was determined to win her back, no matter who might stand in his way.

Though the lodge felt small to him now, it felt empty without any form of companionship. He had grown in the last few years, from an orphan spurning all the affection and friendship that the village and people of the manor readily offered him for solitude and a life in the woods, to a man who was ready to accept the responsibility of his father's name.

He had thought that he was ready to marry Lady Sarah, become the next Lord of Grangeback and accept his place in wider society, but the loss of their child had caused the deep fears of abandonment and loss he still felt to surface. Instead of facing these fears, he gave into them and ran, abandoning them first rather than being abandoned.

It had taken weeks, and the wisdom of Wilbraham Egerton to help him see what a fool he was. When he had received word that Lady Sarah was in danger, he had rushed home, only to find that the danger had passed and it had been Wilbraham that had been the one to protect her in his place.

Mr Hunter knew that he owed a great debt to Wilbraham, one that he could never fully repay. But he could start by at least trying to live up to his obligations.

He had spent the weeks he had been back in Stickleback Hollow pondering what exactly those obligations were whilst he unpacked a handful of items to make the lodge livable.

The time he did not spend in the lodge, he spent foraging and fishing so that he did not have to show his face in the village. His hunting dog, Pattinson, had stayed at Grangeback in the care of Lady Sarah.

When Mr Hunter had departed unexpectedly, he had left the dog behind and it was now more Lady Sarah's pet than it had ever been his. Partly because of how gentle and loving she was with the animal, and partly because Cooky spoiled the dog far more than Mr Hunter ever had.

The luxury of Grangeback was something even an Akita would not readily give up for the cramped conditions of the lodge and hard living in the woods.

He had spent the last few nights out in the woods and was making his way back to the lodge to try and heat some of the cold from his bones. It was slowly getting warmer, but every few days he had to return to the lodge to sleep in a warm bed, wash his clothing and sit by the fire for a few hours.

He rarely used the front door of the lodge, even before Lady Sarah arrived in the village, and now was no exception. The groundskeeper approached the lodge from the rear and open the small door which led into the kitchen.

It took a moment for his eyes to adjust to the darkness inside, but as they did, he realised that there was a fire burning in the grate and he was not alone in the lodge.

"You certainly have taken your time out there," Brigadier George Webb-Kneelingroach said in a dry tone, not shifting his gaze from the hearth he was sitting beside.

"Father, you're back," was all Alex could muster as the hunter tried to hide his surprise at seeing the Lord of Grangeback sat in the lodge.

"Indeed I am," the brigadier replied curtly.

"How long have you been waiting?" Alex asked

with a slight frown as he put down his fishing pole, bow and gun on the small table in the kitchen.

"A day, perhaps a little more. It is hard to tell in a house with no clocks. I, fortunately, had some tea that I brought back with me and some rations I acquired during my journey home. It seems though, you have been away for far longer than that," George said as he turned to face his son for the first time.

There was a look of disappointment in his eyes that Mr Hunter had never seen before, a look that pierced his heart and compounded the guilt he felt.

"I see you have heard rumours of my recent behaviour then," Alex said with a sigh and slowly made his way over to occupy the empty seat that sat opposite his father.

"I have, but I would hear whether it is a mere rumour from you. If there is truth in it, then I would hear that too. I am your father, and I do not wish you would hide anything from me," the brigadier said earnestly as he leaned toward his son.

"Then tell me the rumours you have heard and I will bear them out or dismiss them," Mr Hunter said with an edge of reticence to his voice.

"I have heard that Lady Sarah was taken to hospital near death, that you drowned yourself in gin, and rather than rush to her bedside, you chose to abandon the village without a word," the brigadier said without emotion; his eyes focused steadily on Alex's face as he spoke.

"The rumours are true. I will not lie to you about my behaviour, nor make excuses for it," Mr Hunter replied helplessly.

"I see. What the rumours do not say is what caused Lady Sarah to be taken to the hospital. Sudden illnesses are common, and to think that a woman you are close to will die, given your history of loss, it is not all surprising that you would turn to drink to cope with your situation. But I fear that there is more to it than that," the brigadier shook his head and looked searchingly at his son.

"What then, do you suspect was the cause of her illness?" Alex asked, swallowing hard, knowing that he could not keep anything from his father for long.

"Was she carrying your child?" the brigadier asked as directly as he could. He had never minced words with Alexander from the moment he was old enough to talk. He would not mince them now.

"She was. There was a witch, kidnappings, something happened to her when she was taken. I do not know whether it was magic or simply the trauma of a crazed man taking her when she was in such a condition, but she lost the child, and then I nearly lost her as well. I couldn't bear to see her like that. I could not -" Alex began but the brigadier held up his hand to quiet him.

"I understand. It is not that I would have done differently, but I would have expected more from you. I assume that you are no longer her chosen suitor? There is no engagement?" the brigadier asked.

"There is not, but I do love her. More than I could have believed, and I will not give up pursuing her," Mr Hunter said firmly.

"Alexander, you are my son, and I love you. But I also must think about Sarah in this. She is my ward, and as such, like a daughter to me. I do not wish to see either of you in pain, but if she were to choose another, I will not forbid their union in your favour," the brigadier warned.

"So you have heard those rumours as well?" Alex shook his head and laughed to himself.

"Mr Brown is a wealthy man, and though American, he would not be a bad partner for her, should she choose him. A much better match than the other suitors that came before you, I should say," the brigadier said with a wry smile.

"It is no wonder that you were called away by the crown for clandestine activities," Alex smiled at his father, "it has taken no time at all for you to find out all that has been happening here in your absence."

"I do not like to return home ill-informed. It can lead to all sorts of uncomfortable situations," the brigadier shrugged. Silence fell between the two men for a few moments, as the paid turned their gazes to the fire and watched the flames slowly eating away at the wood within the grate.

"Do you want me to put an end to my intentions towards Sarah?" Alex asked with a feeling of dread in his chest.

"No, I do not think that is necessary, but I would have you prepare yourself. If she does choose another, I do not want you to feel she has ill-used you, or that it is anyone's fault but your own," the brigadier replied.

"I am prepared, father, but I can still hope that there is a way forward for us," Alex shrugged.

"I hope so too, my son," the brigadier said warmly and reached out his hand to pat Mr Hunter's knee, "Now, tell me of all the things that you saw in the northern country. I have no news of anything there," George said, with a twinkle in his eye.

Chapter 4

Lady Sarah listened to the messengers and then retreated to the study. The others would make the necessary preparations without her getting in the way. She would join the others for dinner, but until then, it would be better for Arwyn to talk to the messengers about news from home and other small pleasantries.

She needed some time to think where she would not be interrupted. It had been nearly a year since Grace and Millie had been kidnapped. She had tried to hold onto the hope that they were still alive, that they would be rescued and brought home. But the longer they were missing with no word the harder it became to remain positive.

When she had been prevented from searching for them both herself and had been told to leave it in the hands of others, her hopes had dwindled. But now there was new hope that after everything she had endured in the last year, she would finally be reunited with her two friends.

There was a gentle knock at the door of the study that roused Lady Sarah from her thoughts.

"Yes?" she answered.

The door slowly opened and Sylvia, her current companion and lady's maid stepped into the study and closed the door behind her.

"Mi'lady, Mrs Bosworth has asked me to pack your things for a trip to Wales. Are you to go alone or am I to go too?" Sylvia asked with a stilted formality. She was not known for her propriety or her sense of place in the world.

The two women had met just before Christmas when they had both been kidnapped and held by a zealot doctor and nurse determined to rid the world of fallen women. Though Lady Sarah was not tarred with the brush of stigma, Sylvia had been.

Lady Sarah had returned to Grangeback and her old life once their ordeal was over, but Sylvia had found herself on the streets of Chester.

A chance meeting had seen the pair reunited and Lady Sarah had offered the vacant position in her household to Sylvia.

But Sylvia had never expected the position to be

permanent. She had spent her life being treated as a disposable item and did not expect Lady Sarah to behave any differently.

When Lady Sarah had offered the position to Sylvia, it had seemed to many in the household and Stickleback Hollow that she had given up on finding her friends. That by hiring another to fill Grace's position, she was finally moving on from the pain of losing them both. But Lady Sarah had no such intentions.

In offering Sylvia a job, she was extending a hand to help someone in great need, someone who would be able to stay on at the great house, even when Grace returned. She was sure that the brigadier would have no objections to her having two lady's maids, though whether it would keep her from stumbling into trouble was something that remained to be seen.

"Of course, you are coming!" Lady Sarah sounded slightly affronted by the question.

"May I speak frankly?" Sylvia sighed and looked at the young lady with a hard stare.

"Please," Lady Sarah replied and indicated that Sylvia should sit in one of the two chairs that sat opposite the desk she sat behind.

"Will I need to look for new employment when we have been to Wales? If so, I would rather not make the trip and take my reference now," Sylvia said, refusing to sit. She held onto the door to help her keep her composure.

"Sylvia, I would never dream of ending your time here with me. If you would rather stay behind at the house than come, I understand. But you have no reason to look for employment elsewhere," Lady Sarah replied gently.

"My Lady, you have been so distracted and so absent from the house, it is hard to know whether I am needed here. You have spent all of your hours outside in the farthest corners of the estate. I have turned Mr Brown away at the door, time and again, telling him you are not home and waiting silently with him in the library for hours when he was hoping you would return. If you are to spend all of your life outside -" Sylvia began, but Lady Sarah cut her off with a wave of her hand.

"Please, sit, Sylvia," the young woman said and waited until her maid had taken the chair she indicated, "I cannot begin to apologise for the position I have put you in over the past few weeks. It was unconscionable rude of me to do so, and I have been avoiding not only my responsibilities but my own emotions as well. But, I do need you here. You have been a greater help to me than you could ever know and I would not want you to feel that you are not valued here. I know that this trip to Wales is sudden, and I know that you also know why we are going. Grace returning here will not mean that you are to leave, or will suddenly find yourself without employment. This is your home until you wish it otherwise. Please, rest easy in my confidence in you," Lady Sarah smiled.

"Very well, I will finish your packing and my own. Mrs Boswoth has a long list of things that must be done before you are ready to leave, I am sure she will keep me occupied until the moment the carriage leaves," Sylvia smiled wryly at Lady Sarah, rose quickly and left the room without another word.

Lady Sarah sank back in her chair and sighed to herself. She knew that word would reach Mr Hunter of their departure sooner or later, and that he would insist on accompanying them to Wales. The thought of travelling with him and sharing in another adventure made her feel tired.

The clock in the study showed it was 8 o'clock, far too early to retire to bed when the house was in such an organised state of chaos. She had no doubt that Mrs Bosworth would keep the servants working until the stroke of 12 and have them up at 4 o'clock again.

She rubbed her temples and considered ringing for tea. Pattinson was in the kitchen begging for scraps and his presence was not missed. Though she loved the animal dearly, there were times when solitude was needed, and it was better that he was under the feet of Cooky.

There was a second knock at the door.

"Yes?" Lady Sarah called out.

The door opened slowly and in the doorway was a welcome surprise, Lady Szonja, Countess of Huntingdon and cousin of the Egerton family. Her fair skin was tinged with the colour of the Indian sun and she looked well for it.

"You're back!" Lady Sarah exclaimed with delight.

"Yes, dear child, we are all home. I suspect that the brigadier will be along shortly, he has been visiting with the doctor and Mr Hunter first. I doubt he would have brought himself to leave here again if he had come to see you first," Szonja smiled and held her arms open to embrace the young lady.

Lady Sarah rushed to the friendly arms and broke down into tears as she was enveloped in them.

"Hush, little one, I know you must have much to tell me, but there is no need for tears," Szonja said warmly, but it did not stem the flow of tears from Lady Sarah.

The pair stood in the study for a few minutes whilst emotion poured out of Lady Sarah. Lady Szonja soothed her friend until the tears abated and then slowly led her over to the two chairs beside the desk.

"Has it really been so bad?" the countess asked with a frown.

Lady Sarah nodded.

"Then let me shut the door, and you can tell me of everything that has happened since we left, and I shall, in turn, tell you of our adventures," Lady Szonja smiled and patted Lady Sarah's hands affectionately before she shut the door to the study and pour Lady Sarah a stiff drink.

"Start from the beginning, it is always the best place," the countess said as she handed over the glass of whisky and sat down to listen to Lady Sarah.

Chapter 5

Stanley and Lee Baker were giddy with excitement as they made their way back to their home. They were still eating meals at the manor, but as the arrival of their mother was imminent they had decided to sleep in their old beds, so they would more than likely be there to welcome her home.

But the thought of travelling to Wales on another adventure with her ladyship had pushed all thought of their mother's return from their minds. They half-skipped, half-ran through the narrow lanes of Stickleback Hollow until they reached the top of the street that their mother's shop stood on.

Miss Angela Baker was not their mother by birth but adoption, and as a successful seamstress, she had been able to keep both boys in good clothes and well-fed in a time when so many orphans were forced into orphanages and half-starved before being cast out into a cruel world that often saw them landed in prison or worse.

It had been sheer luck that Lee and Stanley Baker had found themselves on her doorstep and she had done all that she could to protect and love the pair from the horrible fate that awaited so many others.

In Stickleback Hollow, it was well known that the pair were not her biological sons, but the boys were unaware of the truth. They were mature in many ways, but it would be a few years before Angela Baker would think they were ready to learn of their parentage.

In truth, she knew little about their biological mother and even less about their father, but before she told them, she would find out all she could so that she could answer any questions they might have.

As the two boys looked down the street, they could see the lamps inside the shop were burning, and for a moment the pair stopped to argue about which of them had left the lamps burning when they had gone back to the manor.

The sound of them arguing filtered down the quiet street and reached the ears of Miss Baker, who smiled at the familiar sound. She was tired from the journey and had been waiting until the morning to go to Grangeback to see her sons.

She rushed to the door and flung it open, calling out into the night,

"I thought I raised you better than to argue in the street!"

The two Baker boys froze mid-argument and turned slowly to see the slightly tanned figure of their mother waiting for them with open arms. The pair did not waste a moment, but rushed, slipping on the frozen patches of water in the street, headlong into their mother, embracing her in a firm hug that all three had been waiting so long for.

"Oh, mother!" Lee cried, his voice muffled as his face was buried in her shoulder.

"We're so happy you are home!" Stanley said in an equally muffled voice.

"It is good to see you both looking so well, I did not expect you to be here, but sleeping at the manor," Miss Baker said as she held her sons.

"We wanted to be here when you got home. Lady Sarah said we still had to eat at the manor but that we could get things ready here for you," Lee explained as he sniffed and turned his head away from his mother.

"I see, well, we should go inside and talk. I want to know about all of your adventures," Miss Baker said as she let the boys go and stepped back into the warmth of the shop.

"What about your adventures? What about Mr Cartwright? We thought he would be here with you," Stanley said as he followed his mother inside and Lee shut the door behind them.

"There is not much I can tell you about my adventures, but Mr Cartwright will not be coming back. He was hurt very badly and if he had tried to return he would have died. I could not stay with him, because I had you to come home to, but he is being well looked after by a friend. He will write to us, but he will not see Stickleback Hollow again," Angela said gently as the three of them settled themselves around the fireside.

"What happened to him?" Lee gasped.

"He was caught by our enemies. Captain Jonnes Smith and the brigadier rescued him, but he had been hurt very badly. I would rather talk of your adventures though. It is very painful to think and speak of Henry still," Miss

Baker replied with tears in her eyes.

"We made some new friends, Charlotte and Charles Egerton, they are just like us! We got into lots of trouble over Christmas. Mrs Bosworth and Lady Egerton were very cross with us," Stanley giggled.

"Did you cause Lady Sarah a lot of trouble?" Angela asked with a raised eyebrow.

"No! We helped her a lot! She was in the hospital for a long time and she was kidnapped, and men came to try and kill her," Lee exclaimed.

"Gracious! I assume they were unsuccessful," Miss Baker said as she listened to her sons describe in great detail all of the events that had taken place in Stickleback Hollow since her departure.

She laughed and gasped in the appropriate places, but kept her own counsel when she heard of Mr Hunter's departure, the arrival of Mr Oliver Henry Brown, and Mr Hunter's return. She suspected the cause of Lady Sarah's hospitalisation, but she did not speak of it to her sons, to whom it seemed a mystery.

The hours ticked by as she listened to them talk and it felt like she had never been away, that she had not had to say goodbye to the man that she loved and leave him behind in the hands of a woman she was unsure she could trust to take care of him.

As they talked, they finally reached the events of the day and the news of their imminent journey to Wales. Miss Baker felt her heart fall as she listened to the pair talk so animatedly about going with Lady Sarah to rescue Grace and Millie, of all the great things they were going to do and how they had to go as Lady Sarah's bodyguards.

She remembered well it had been her sons that had foiled the first attempt to kidnap the two boys, that without them the two women would have been taken and would have disappeared for good.

But it did not mean that she was ready to say goodbye to her sons after reuniting with them for so short a time. They had grown so much since she had been away, though it had been less than a year.

They were closer to being men than children, and she knew that she could not forbid them or prevent them from going on such a journey, no matter how much she wished they would stay with her in the safety of the seamstress shop.

The boys were not asking her permission to go either, but merely telling her of what adventure they were to go on next.

Instead of voicing the pain she felt, she feigned enthusiasm, knowing that if she mentioned her own thoughts, feelings and plans on the matter, she would guilt her sons into staying with her, something they would surely come to resent her for.

She smiled and made notes of all the things they would need to take with them, and helped them to pack, late into the night. When the boys were too tired to keep their eyes open, she finished what remained to be done and put the trunk at the door to the house, so that it would be easy to collect when the carriage called for them.

She then sat by the fire and mulled over whether she was right in returning to the village, and what the future might hold for her. She could have asked the brigadier to take care of her sons, but it would have led them to feel abandoned. She could have sent for them and given them a new and exciting life in India. But she had not considered returning to Stickleback Hollow to explain she was leaving to take care of Mr Cartwright. Now it was an option for her to consider, and one that would change not only her future but that of her sons as well.

Chapter 6

Edryd felt a weight had been lifted off his shoulders after the two men set off on their journey in the dead of night. No one had seen them go and with instructions not to stop, he had been certain they would both make it through.

A telegram had arrived from Arwyn a day later that read:

Father,

Your guests arrived safely

Your loving son

It was not much as far as messages went, but it was all Edryd needed to know. He knew his son understood the need for secrecy. He also knew that Derwyn would have phrased the message somewhat differently.

The receipt of the telegram had led to Bronwyn asking many questions, all of which Edryd had dismissed with a wave of his hand and a promise that he would explain later.

He knew that Arwyn would send him another telegram before they departed and that it would tell him how many people to expect, but until then, there was nothing more to worry about. He spent the day on his farm, out on the sunlight that warmed his skin and showed that spring was only a few weeks away.

The spring flowers were already beginning to show their shoots above the melting snow and the patches of ice that could still be found in certain areas of the farmyard and the pathways that wove their way between the fields of Edryd's ancestral home.

He and the farmhands were out in the fields all day, preparing for the lambing that was to come, moving the sheep carrying lambs to the pastures close to the house and the other ewes were shepherded to another field where they could be kept away from the chaos that was about to unfold.

A few days before the ewes were due to lamb, they would be taken into the large barn so that they could give birth in warm hay instead of on the frozen ground.

There was a great deal of work that went into the welcoming the new lives into the world, and it would be a few days of sleepless nights with at least one of the farmhands staying up all night with the ewes, but aside from taking a few hours to sleep each day, Edryd rarely left his sheep during this time.

Bronwyn did not take part in the preparation for lambing but was the mother that abandoned lambs would be adopted by. Every life was precious on the farm, and the pair had never lost a lamb that they could help.

There were occasions when they arrived too late to save a lamb or one was birthed already passed on, but those were the tragedies of life that they could do nothing about.

Bronwyn spend her time during lambing preparation knitting coats for the lambs that would be brought into her charge. She often laughed at the irony that the wool she used to make the coats were probably from the very ewes that were abandoning their young.

She often had wry thoughts that Edryd could not fathom the source of, but it was one of the things that made her such an interesting individual to him.

As the night drew in, Edryd sent the men back to their homes to suppers that would warm their cold bones after a day of hard work and similarly made his way back to the farmhouse.

He expected to see the welcoming lights of home in the distance, but there was only the light from the common lodging-house shining in the darkness.

Edryd frowned at the lack of light but thought it was possible that Bronwyn had fallen asleep whilst knitting at some time in the afternoon and had not roused herself yet to light the lamps and cook their evening meal.

He made his way to the backdoor by the kitchen, kicked off his boots outside and opened the door. The house was completely still, there was no sound of heavy breathing or snoring that he had expected to hear. But it was not the lack of sound that caused Edryd to freeze in the doorway.

The smell of blood was heavy in the air, sickly and filled with iron, a scent he was all too familiar with from when they had to slaughter one of their animals.

His mind was a fog as he tried to decide what to do. If he stepped into the house alone, there was no telling what he would find and if he would be able to leave in order to call for help.

But if Bronwyn was in danger, going for help first could mean that he would be too late when he reached her.

There was a fire bell that stood a few feet from the back door, mounted to the side of the house. Every building in the farmyard had one. In a world of wood, straw and living creatures, a fire spread quickly and killed effectively. If the alarm wasn't raised quickly, lives were lost. So Edryd had made sure that the bells were positioned everywhere and that everyone on the farm knew how to use them.

He didn't bother with his boots and barely noticed the freezing ground beneath his feet as he stepped out of the doorway and with all his might, rang the bell.

It took a few moments before the men began streaming out of the common lodging-house looking everywhere for the source of the fire.

Spotting Edryd by the main house, they rushed towards him. The sight of him shoeless in the freezing weather was enough to convince the men that this was more than a practice drill.

"One of you go for the doctor," Edryd gasped as he stopped ringing the bell. One of the men nodded and set off directly. He did not need to be asked twice and hurried to the barn to throw a bridle on one of the horses and rode out moments later, without a saddle, pushing the horse as much as he dared to in the frozen conditions.

The other men stayed with Edryd and followed him into the house. The smell of blood struck each of them in turn as they passed through the doorway and entered the dark of the house.

One of the men took it upon himself to light the lamps in each room as they searched. The kitchen was void of any signs of blood or of Bronwyn, as was the sitting room and the dining room. The study was empty too, and the drawing room. They searched the downstairs rooms thoroughly to no avail before they turned their attention to the upper floor.

The farmhouse remained quiet and still save for the sounds of the men moving about. None of them spoke as they searched. There was no need for them to speak about the horrors that were filling their minds. At best one of the animals had been slaughtered in the house, and the worst, the worst did not bear thinking about.

Edryd made his way down the corridor towards the

door to his bedroom. The scent of blood was stronger up here and the closer he drew to the bedroom, the more intense the scent became.

He did not know what waited for him behind the door, but he knew that he had to go through it, no matter what sight awaited him.

As he pushed the door open the overwhelming scent of spilt blood rushed into his nostrils. The scent was enough to turn the stomach of most men, but it was something that Edryd had learned to cope with and push past. Nausea rumbled in the depths of his belly, but it was not the scent of blood that was responsible for the feeling.

On the bed, lay his wife, Bronwyn, her face battered and bruised and her eyes firmly shut. There was no blood on her body and she looked like she was dead. The scent of blood was animal blood. One of the ewes that had been brought down to lamb lay on the floor of the room, its blood coating the boards, and a message was scrawled on the wall in its blood.

But Edryd did not see the ewe or the message, he only saw his wife. He rushed to her side, slipping on the blood as he went.

"Bronwyn!" He cried out, and to his relief, she stirred on the bed and said something that he could not understand.

The men of the farm stood at the door looking up at the wall, the message scrawled there:

Do not interfere in matters that do not concern you.

Chapter 7

To say Grace was tired, would be akin to saying that your feet hurt after walking from Land's End to John o'Groats.

She did not know how long it had been since she had been taken from the bonfire banquet in Stickleback Hollow. She could not remember the faces of her friends or the sound of their voices. She had struggled so hard to escape in the first few weeks, but now she was just tired.

It had been some time since she had stopped trying to escape and had accepted that her life was different now. She did not know where Millie was. It had been so long since she had seen her friend that it almost didn't matter where she was or what had happened to her. For now, Grace was alive and the two men that held her had shown no indication that her life was at risk.

She was given three meals a day, a blanket to sleep under at night, and clothes that kept her warm during the day. There was nothing else.

It had been three months before she had learned the names of the two men that held her J D Beets and Thae J. Land.

But once she knew their names, all hope of being released or allowed to escape was gone. There was no possibility that they would allow her to go knowing their names. It was too much of a risk.

If she did try to escape, it would be tantamount to a death sentence. So, Grace accepted her lot in life and even began to come accustomed to the routine of life with the two men. She had not seen hide nor hair of Millie since the first week that the pair had been abducted.

Grace concluded that the reason for their separation was that they were less likely to attempt an escape. If one left the other behind, the other would be in danger, so it had kept them both obedient and submissive.

There was no evidence that Millie was even alive as far as Grace could tell, but she could not bring herself to attempt escape, even with those thoughts settled in her mind. In her heart, she knew she had no evidence that Millie was dead, and therefore any attempt to leave on her part was the same as killing Millie with her own two hands.

When she had finally accepted her imprisonment, finally become compliant with their wishes, the two men had given her more scope to move about, in fact, they had left the cave that they had held the two women in and moved into an old house that sat in a small clearing.

It had been the dead of night when they had moved and only J D Beets had been with her when they moved. She imagined that Thae J. Land was with Millie, and it had been the only form of confirmation that she had to indicate that Millie still lived.

In the house, she was given the run of certain rooms and the penalties for leaving those rooms were outlined to her in great detail. There was no reason to doubt their sincerity and she knew that her life was infinitely easier when she obeyed the instruction she was given.

But it all left her tired to the very core of her being. It had been so long since she had felt any form of emotion that she wasn't sure what they were anymore. She did not fear the two men, though she knew they were dangerous and held her life in their hands. She did not experience any form of happiness in her daily life, there was the day and the tasks she was set - cooking, cleaning, and even sometimes out in the small garden that lay at the back of the house surrounded by a stone wall - but none of it made her happy.

She had vague memories of her life before she had been kidnapped, very slight impressions of emotions that she had once known, but she did not let her mind wander to her memories very often. Grace had fought with all her might to hold onto those memories in the beginning, but the longer she had clung to faint hope, the more unbearable her captivity was.

When she had finally locked the door to her memories and emotions, she had been able to survive, able to get through each day. There were times when she didn't know what would be worse - a living death of simply existing, or death itself - but in her living death, there was the faint promise that one day, she might once again feel again.

Neither J D nor Thae paid much attention to Grace anymore. She was simply there as a means to an end. They were rarely together in the rooms that she was allowed to occupy, but when they were, they discussed plans that she couldn't help but listen to.

"Has the boss said anything about our moving yet?" Thae asked one evening as Grace was serving their evening meal.

"Nuffink, I fink we're stuck in this rotten place for a while," J D had shrugged in response.

"I thought we were bound for the Americas, hiding amongst the hive of people that arrive there every day," Thae sighed and looked out the window at the miserable weather outside the window.

The day had started with bright sun but as the evening had worn on, a storm had blown in. The windows of the house rattled as the wind whipped around them and the wooden beams in the roof creaked as the old house groaned against the wind.

"We were, but there were too many of those nosy bastards looking for the women. We've got to sit tight until they've been dealt with or they've given up looking," J D replied between mouthfuls of the mashed potato that Grace was piling on his plate.

"Did you take care of the issue today?" Thae asked with a slight sigh.

"I did. Should be the end of that. The stupid cow

tried to fight back. Stabbed one of the guys with a knitting needle. Couldn't get it out again, so had to do away wif him in the woods. Left the others to bury him. Fink they'll all be a bit more careful in future. But won't be that long now til we get rid of them. Boss doesn't want any loose ends," J D replied with a malicious grin.

"It had to be the woman?" Thae asked with a raised eyebrow. He was an educated man who worked for his employer for ideological reasons. He could be counted on to do jobs that others would not due to a strong constitution, but he was not pleased with his association with a man such as J D.

J D Beets was a man who simply enjoyed violence. It did not matter to him whom he had to hurt, only that he was allowed to hurt them. The more violent the assignment, the better. He was closer to a mindless beast than a man, but he had his uses, at least to his employer. He was always willing to do the tasks that required a lack of conscience. Something he had been conveniently born without.

Unlike Thae, he had no education, and though he found the company of a man that was so rigid and proper irritating, he knew better than to meat out violence when it had not been requested by his boss.

Thae longed to leave England and had been only too glad to take on the job of kidnapping as it came with the promise of a new life in America. But it had been many months of waiting, so long that he was beginning to believe that he would be stuck in the wet and miserable wilds forever.

He did not talk about what had brought his life to such a place, or what forces were pressuring him to leave, but it was clear, even to someone like J D that he was growing more anxious to leave with every passing day.

"She was the one in the house. The man wasn't there, but always a better message when you hurt the women. Men know that you'll do far worse to them," J D shrugged.

"Then we'll have to wait and see. If you've done all you can, then we should be leaving here before the end of winter. The sooner we go, the better," Thae said spitefully and the two men lapsed into silence as they ate.

Grace moved out of the room silently and for the first time in several months, she was overwhelmed with sadness at the thought of leaving her homeland. So much so, that the moment she arrived back in her bedroom, she sank to her knees in tears and began to pray.

Please, God, don't let them take me from here.

Please.

Chapter 8

The brigadier arrived at the manor just as Arwyn was leaving. The constable was surprised to see the Lord of Grangeback returned and in such good health.

"Come, stay awhile," the brigadier encouraged the policeman but Arwyn shook his head.

"I must go speak to Mr Hunter. I am afraid this shall not be much of a homecoming for you," Arwyn sighed and made to continue outside.

"What on earth has happened?" the brigadier asked with a furrowed brow.

"I think it best if you speak to Lady Sarah. You have two guests for the night, I will be back shortly with Mr Hunter, but I find it unlikely that we will stay the whole night," Arwyn sighed and hurried on his way.

George did not delay the young constable any longer but let him disappear into the thick dark of the ailing winter.

As he stepped into the entrance hall he felt a great sense of relief at finally being home. He had returned safely from the dangers of his mission for the crown and could finally enjoy the years he had remaining, reconciled with his son and blessed with a young ward.

But it became clear all too soon that the manor was far from peaceful. The servants rushed by, barely registering that he was there.

Mrs Bosworth was nowhere to be seen and Bosworth was not at his usual post.

The brigadier walked through the great house to the kitchen where Cooky was yelling orders at everyone in sight. Pattinson was snoozing by the backdoor, a comfortable spot that was out of the main flow of the kitchen traffic but in a prime position to garner treats from Cooky every time she passed.

It was Pattinson that was the first to notice the brigadier, and the Akita pelted full tilt from the backdoor to the brigadier's side, barking excitedly and sending severally of the scullery maids flying.

"At least I was missed by one amongst the house," George laughed as he knelt beside the dog and scratched behind his ears.

Pattinson barked excitedly and licked the brigadier's face.

"Brigadier!" Cooky screeched and all activity in the kitchen ground to a sudden halt as the staff lined up to welcome their lord and master home.

One of the maids that Pattinson had thrown aside in his great hurry to greet the brigadier, disappeared from the kitchen and returned moments later with Mrs Bosworth in tow.

There were twenty minutes of greetings and exchanging of pleasantries until Mrs Bosworth steered the brigadier from the kitchen and the activity there immediately resumed.

"Would someone tell me what has happened that has caused such activity?" the brigadier asked Mrs Bosworth as the pair walked towards the study.

"We have had news that Grace and Millie have been found. Everyone is preparing to set out to rescue them," Mrs Bosworth said shortly.

"I see, and where is Bosworth, I would have expected to see him here," George said with a slight affront.

"He has gone to fetch the doctor and his sons. Richard and Gordon have yet to depart following Christmas. They have both graduated from University and have been looking for employment in London. It has not been easy for Gordon especially and the pair decided to spend a little extra time with their father following the events over Christmas," Mrs Bosworth explained.

"I see, I have only heard Mr Hunter's account of events since I left. I was hoping that I would have some time with my ward, but it seems that she will only be here for a matter of hours," the brigadier sighed.

"She is in the study with the Countess of Huntingdon at present, I am sure that they will both be glad of your company," Mrs Bosworth replied.

"Mrs Bosworth, I wish you to speak freely. Is Lady Sarah well?" the brigadier asked with genuine affection and pain in his voice.

"She is as well as anyone could be. She has made some valuable friends and hurt her enemies greatly. She will recover, but I do not know if she will ever be able to love as she once did," Mrs Bosworth said sadly with a shake of her head.

"I understand, thank you. And thank you for all that you have done in my absence," the brigadier offered her a warm smile that they both knew hid the sadness he felt for his ward.

"I did no more than my duty demanded, but you are welcome," Mrs Bosworth replied with a slight curtsy before she left the brigadier and resumed her overseeing of room preparation and packing.

The brigadier slowly opened the door to the study and stepped inside without announcing himself. Lady Sarah was still in the arms of Lady Szonja, her face red from all the tears spilt. No words needed to be said. The brigadier walked briskly over to his ward and held her as a father holds his daughter to keep her from harm.

"I am so glad you are home," Lady Sarah sighed after a few moments.

"So am I, dear girl, so am I,' the brigadier replied.

~*~*~

Arwyn did not waste any time in his mission to inform Mr Hunter of the news from his father and of the plans to go to Wales.

It had passed midnight before the two men reached

the manor with Mr Hunter's belongings. Arwyn did not need to pack, his father still had many of his clothes that had been left behind when Arwyn had run away from home to find his place in Stickleback Hollow.

The two messengers had been sleeping for several hours when the two men arrived at the house. Lady Sarah, the countess and the brigadier had spent their time locked in the study talking of everything that they had seen and heard whilst they had been parted.

Sylvia was introduced to them both, and the brigadier welcomed her warmly to the household.

It was decided that Lady Sarah's horse would be ridden by Arwyn and Mr Hunter would take Harald as their mounts. The two riders would take two of the other horses from the stables and they would leave before there was any sight of light in the sky.

The group would make for the Evans farm as quickly as they could and they would investigate the situation before the others arrived.

Derwyn arrived back at the manor to a flurry of activity and the news that they were all bound for his home. The moment he heard, he left directly and returned with

Miss DeVille and the assertion that they would both be making the journey.

Gordon had not delayed in accompanying Bosworth to Grangeback to find out all he could about what was happening. The doctor and Richard took longer to pack for the journey and arrived at the manor in the doctor's trap at 1 o'clock in the morning.

Besides the riders, no one in the house had slept. But as the preparations came to a close, Mrs Bosworth made sure that the staff were all in bed before 2 o'clock and impressed upon them that they would not be expected to rise before 8 o'clock.

The trunk that Mr Hunter had packed was put with the luggage that would be transported in the carriage and at 3 o'clock in the morning, Arwyn, the two messengers and the groundskeeper set off on their long journey back to Wales.

The night swallowed them in moments, and each of those left waiting on the steps of the manor said a silent prayer for their safety.

No one left the manor that night. Mrs Bosworth had prepared rooms so that all could remain there, ready to depart as soon as they were ready. Sleep was hard but not impossible as thoughts and emotions swirled inside each of their minds, but when they did finally sleep, their nights were peaceful.

Though it was 8 o'clock when the household staff began their days, it was 10 o'clock before the household rose from their beds and breakfast was served in the dining room.

Miss Baker, Stanley and Lee Baker were all waiting at the house long before the first of them stirred.

The brigadier was the first to rise, the comfort of his own bed alien after the long absence from it and the conditions that he had become accustomed to in India and China.

Breakfast was a solemn affair that was interrupted by the unexpected arrival of Mr Oliver Henry Brown, Mr Edward Egerton and Mr Thomas Egerton.

To find the house so full and their mother's cousin returned was a surprise to the three gentlemen.

"We never expected to see so many here this morning, what party have we missed?" Edward Egerton asked with a great smile as the three gentlemen entered the dining room.

"Good morning, won't you join us?" the brigadier offered.

"I think we could suffer through a second breakfast of some description," Thomas Egerton beamed as he greedily went to inspect the contents of the silver breakfast platters on the sideboard that ran parallel to the dining table.

"And who might this gentleman be?" the brigadier asked as he pointed his fork in the direction of Mr Brown.

"May I present our cousin, recently arrived from the Americas, Mr Oliver Henry Brown," Edward said grandly, "Oliver, this is the Brigadier, George Webb-Kneelingroach, master of this great house and guardian of the beautiful Lady Sarah."

"Flattery at breakfast?" Lady Sarah asked with mock exasperation.

"Flattery is a fine accompaniment to any meal," Edward shrugged with a smile.

"So what solemn occasion has caused such a quiet feast between such great friends?" Thomas asked he sat down beside the doctor at the far end of the table.

"There is no occasion," Mr Hunter shrugged.

"Come now, doctor, to have such a group gathered at one table and there to be nothing but long faces, there is something surely amiss!" Edward said disbelievingly.

"We are departing for Wales as soon as the carriage is packed. We have had word of Grace and Millie and are headed at once to see what can be done," Lady Sarah replied.

"I see, then Hunter and the good constable are not joining you on this great adventure?" Edward asked with a wry smile, casting his eyes toward his cousin.

"They left last night to scout ahead of the party," Lady Szonja said with an eyebrow raised archly in the direction of Edward.

"Are you all bound on this mission of rescue?" Oliver asked with all the innocence he could muster.

"No, the countess, Miss Baker, and I shall not be joining the group. We have not long returned from our own adventures overseas and we shall be taking the time to rest in the peace and quiet of an empty manor," the brigadier replied gruffly.

"Well then, I would say that it is the perfect

coincidence that we came to call! The ladies are still at court in London, so we are at something of a loose end. If it would please the brigadier and Lady Sarah, we can accompany you without delay on your mission of mercy," Edward said grandly and Thomas shovelled another forkful of food into his mouth.

"Do you not need to pack?" the doctor frowned.

"We can go home directly, pack and be back here within a few hours," Thomas grunted.

"The more the merrier than," Richard said jovially and clapped Edward on the shoulder.

"Excellent, excellent, we shall away at once and be ready for you presently," Edward replied with a grin. Thomas mournfully put down his fork and leaving behind only a small amount of scrambled egg on his plate, rose and followed his brother and cousin from the dining room.

Lady Sarah did not say a word or let the mask of serenity slip from her face. After successfully avoiding both Oliver and Alex for several weeks, she was now bound to Wales with both men.

For the sake of Millie and Grace, she was glad that so many were willing to risk untold dangers to rescue them, so rather than worrying about her own awkwardness, she chose to focus on the positives for her friends.

"What a group we shall be!" Stanley Baker said brightly from his seat.

The doctor inwardly groaned and half-wished he had the good sense to stay behind in Stickleback Hollow rather than join the expedition filled with impetuous youths. If it were not for his son, Gordon, and not knowing what they would find when they reached Wales, he knew that he would have gladly stayed home and settled back into the quiet of his house and practice in the village.

"Indeed," the brigadier said, and conversation ceased again. The bright energy that the Egertons had brought to the dining room faded quickly, as each returned to their own thoughts, worries and apprehensions about the task that lay before them.

For Gordon, he had only one focus, to bring Millie home with him, no matter what it might cost.

Chapter 9

The rest of Breakfast passed in silence. The carriages were packed and goodbyes were said to Cooky, Mrs Bosworth, the brigadier, Bosworth, Miss Baker and the countess.

There had been an extremely long conversation about whether Pattinson should accompany the party or remain behind at the house, but ultimately, Lady Sarah wanted the dog with her, and no amount of pouting by Cooky could change her ladyship's mind.

The dog happily jumped into the carriage behind the young lady and settled on the bench next to her. The Baker Boys and the doctor were her other companions for the journey.

The brigadier had ordered the three large carriages that belonged to the Manor to be readied for the journey. Each carriage had four horses in a team and the expedition had all but emptied the stables of Grangeback.

Only three horses remained in the stables. One was the doctor's horse for his trap and the other two belonged to the two messengers. The brigadier and Edryd would make arrangements over the swapped animals when the escapade to rescue Grace and Millie was over. But for the moment, the two animals were resting well in the luxurious surroundings of the large stables, and frolicking in the large open paddocks.

The second carriage held Richard, Gordon, Edward, Thomas, Oliver and Derwyn. It was the largest of the carriages but even so, the men felt it was a tight squeeze with all six of them seated inside.

The final carriage was the smallest of them and contain Silvia and Miss DeVille. The two women had the most space to enjoy as the carriages lurched along the driveway of Grangeback and began the long, slow journey to Wales.

It did not take long for Edward, Thomas and Oliver to return with their luggage, which was quickly stowed and their own carriage was driven back to Tatton Park without delay.

There was no entourage to wish the men well on

their quest, and Lady Sarah suspected they had not told another soul where they were headed.

As the afternoon wore on, it became evident that they would need to stop for something to eat. Though most of the party had eaten well at the late breakfast, the horses needed rest and Lady Sarah was adamant that Pattinson should be allowed to get out of the carriage to find a tree.

It was 3 o'clock in the afternoon and the party had not yet left the boundaries of Cheshire. There was an inn close to the Welsh border that had a yard large enough to accommodate the three carriages.

It was called The Red Lyon and lay in the quiet farming village of Dodleston. The Welsh border was not far so it seemed the ideal location for the party to sup at.

The landlord was astonished at the sight of so many carriages arriving at once and thrilled that food and drinks were required by all. The grooms rushed out to tend to the horses and the drivers were brought food and drinks in the yard so that they could stay with the carriages and the luggage.

Pattinson was greatly relieved to be able to escape the confines of the carriage and made sure that he made the most of the small amount of freedom he was granted.

"Not often do we see such people travelling this way," the landlord said as he served plates of cheese, cold meats, bread and butter to the group.

"We are going to visit a dear friend," Lady Sarah replied with a smile. She was well aware that their party was suspicious, and would be made to look even more so if no explanation was forthcoming.

"Ah, then that would explain it. I'd be wary around here though, been highwaymen spotted on the road. Viscous group robbing anyone they can. I wouldn't want ya to find yaselves in trouble now," the landlord replied.

"Highwaymen?" the doctor asked.

"That seems odd these days," Richard agreed.

"As long as ya got men without work and a way to feed their young 'uns, you'll have thieves and highwaymen. The closest thing we have here to law is all the way in Chester. Too far out for them to bother too much with us here, not in a place with mostly farmhands being the rotten ones. Farmers soon sort out the ones that cause problems and we have our own form of justice here if they step out of line," the landlord replied with a toothy grin.

"Have the highwaymen bothered the farms or just travellers?" Lady Sarah asked with piqued curiosity.

"So far just travellers, mi'lady. And there's been none coming round spending more than they ought to, so it's none of the lads working the farms behind it," the landlord shrugged.

"I see, where have most of the attacks been taking place?" the young lady asked and both Thomas and Edward let out a heavy sigh.

"If there is a mystery to be found, it always finds you," Richard laughed.

"Ah, fancy yaselves mystery solvers do ya? Well, I don't condone putting pretty ladies in danger, but I will tell you that there is a stretch of trees that run either side of the road as you turn towards Hawarden over the border that seems to be where most of the attacks are happening. If yer as smart as you look, then you'll find another road," the landlord advised.

He left the party to their meals, but it was evident from the look in Lady Sarah's eye that their arrival at the farm of the Evans family would be delayed a little longer.

It was dark by the time the carriages pulled out of

the yard of the Red Lyon and finally crossed the border into Wales.

The drivers had been given explicit instructions to follow the road towards Hawarden and keep their eyes open for anything suspicious.

Pattinson was sat next to Lady Sarah in her carriage at the front of the convoy. His ears were pricked and his eyes alert but he gave no hint of any danger lurking in the trees. The group reached Hawarden just before six o'clock but decided to go no further that evening.

They found rooms for the night at the Fox and Grapes Inn. The luggage was brought out of the carriages and piled into their rooms. Miss DeVille, Lady Sarah and Sylvia had a large room to themselves that Pattinson would sleep in with them.

Derwyn, Richard and Gordon had a room together, the doctor was forced to assume responsibility for the Baker Boys, and the three men of Tatton Park had the final room.

The beds were not as comfortable as the majority of the party were used to, but they were clean, it was dry and warm.

The food was good and hearty, the beer weak and

warming, but it was a welcome evening repast for the group. They passed the evening pleasantly, talking of nothing in particular as they sat around their tables, but listening intently to the other conversations in the tavern.

There was talk of the highwaymen, but nothing that could help the group to know where they were supposed to search.

After the group had eaten, Lady Sarah stood from the table and declared,

"Pattinson has been cooped up all day, it is time he had some exercise. I will be back presently," she smiled.

"I think to go walking alone at night would be a mistake, my lady, I will accompany you," Sylvia said with a slightly raised eyebrow. She knew full well that the dog was just an excuse for the lady to slip away and search the woods for signs of highwaymen - something Sylvia was not about to let Lady Sarah do alone.

"We'll come too!" the Baker boys volunteered in one voice as they leapt from their seats and bounded towards the door.

"I think I could use the exercise as well, but the rest of you should rest here by the fire," Richard smiled and patted his father reassuringly on the shoulder.

"A wise idea, my son, but be careful out in the dark," the doctor warned.

Oliver began to rise to volunteer to be part of the expedition in the dark, but both Thomas and Edward took hold of him and pulled him back to his seat before he could speak.

"What are you doing?" he hissed at his cousins as Lady Sarah and her companions made their way across the tavern floor.

"Keeping yourself from looking a fool," Thomas replied, but said no more, instead he turned to Derwyn to question him about growing up in Wales.

Outside the night was cool and dark but t was filled with noise from the small village. Pattinson was excited to be walking in a new place with new smells to explore. He scampered about the streets, glad that there was a lack of heavy traffic to run him down. Sylvia walked beside Richard and the Baker boys walked arm-in-arm with Lady Sarah.

They looked like an odd group as they made their way out of the village and back toward the line of trees they had been told were home to the highwaymen.

Lady Sarah knew full well she had fooled no one about her true intent, but she was also glad that only a small group of them came to investigate this particular mystery.

Richard had the foresight of mind to have borrowed three lanterns from the inn to light their path as they left the warm glow of the village.

The forest was dark and still save for the light from the lanterns and the sound of their footsteps crunching through the snow.

There had not been any fresh snowfall for days, so it was easy to see where people had been walking between the trees. It was a light dusting on the ground, but enough to show the footprints of what looked to be two men leading from the road off into the woods.

Pattinson carefully examined the footprints before he let out a short bark and began scampering along the trail into the darkness.

"We better get after him," Richard sighed and with the two Baker boys at his side and one of the lanterns in his hand, he jogged after the dog.

Lady Sarah and Sylvia followed the path of prints

left behind the group, walking carefully, each holding a lantern to keep the shadows around them at bay.

It was not a long way through the trees to the end of the trail, but there were some rather difficult patches of low hanging branches and thickets to traverse.

As the two women caught up to the others, they found Pattinson sitting outside the entrance to a small cave that was almost invisible in the darkness until you were on top of it.

Stanley Baker stood next to the dog holding his collar to make sure he did not rush off inside.

"Where are Richard and Lee?" Lady Sarah asked.

"They are inside, they told me to wait here for you you and make Pattinson stand guard," Stanley explained.

"You will need this then," Lady Sarah said as she handed over her lantern, "If Pattinson barks, come in at once and tell us. Pattinson, guard," Lady Sarah said firmly to the pair before she and Sylvia ducked inside the cave.

"What treasure have you discovered?" Sylvia asked dryly as she held up the lantern to try and see further inside the cave.

"Supplies, lots of them. And signs that someone was

living here for a while. Maybe three of four people," Richard replied from further inside the cave.

"Does it look like plunder?" Lady Sarah asked, only half-joking.

"Not at all. I doubt very much there ever were any highwaymen but a ruse created to keep people from venturing too deep into the trees and finding this hiding spot," Richard replied.

"How strange, I wonder who would keep supplies in a cave like this so close to a village," Sylvia frowned as she joined Lee and helped him lift the lid off one of the barrels at the back of the cave.

"Another piece of a mystery to be solved," Richard shrugged with a smile.

Before Lady Sarah could reply there was a scrambling sound behind them as Stanley scrambled into the cave.

"Stanley, where is Pattinson?" Lady Sarah frowned at the boy.

"I don't know, he started whining and then wrenched himself free and ran off!" Stanley looked like he was about to cry.

"I wouldn't worry about him," a familiar voice replied from the mouth of the cave and Pattinson barked excitedly.

Chapter 10

On their hard ride in the dark hours, the four riders had made only one stop. At the police house on the outskirts of Chester where Constable McGill and Constable McIntyre could be found. With the return of Captain Jonnes Smith, and what he knew would be a time filled with confusion and some rather swift punishments for indiscretions in his absence, there would be no excuse for him abandoning Stickleback Hollow without finding someone to stand in for him.

Constable McGill readily agreed, and Constable McIntyre went to fetch Constable Cantello from the police station in the centre of the city to ensure that should Constable McGill would have support should he need it.

With a policeman for the village secured, the party did not dally. They rode until the sun began to rise and then stopped just over the border in Boughton at The Waterloo Arms to rest and eat. All four men were tired by the time they finally reached the farm, but there was not a soul to be found in the yard. The two riders led Arwyn and Alex to an empty room in the common lodging-house to rest for a few hours before they rode out again to begin their search.

All four men slept longer than intended, as when they woke the sky was already beginning to darken. Still, there was no one in the common lodging-house and no signs of life in the farmhouse.

The two riders and Arwyn seemed unconcerned by the lack of movement in the yard, but something about it unsettled Alex greatly.

"It's nearly lambing season, they'll be working until the light comes back into the sky to get things ready," Arwyn had shrugged when Alex had asked about it, but still the hunter was unconvinced.

The four men ate heartily before they re-saddled their horses and made their way out into the gathering night.

"It's a short ride, but we shouldn't push the horses too hard now, not after the ride to get here," one of the riders had said and it was agreed that they would go no faster than a walk.

Arwyn and one of the riders each carried a lantern on a crook so that they could hold the reins and see along the road ahead of them.

They made good time as they passed the village of Hawarden and headed off the road into a clump of trees. The men gave their horses their heads and allowed them to pick their way through the trees and over the scrub on the ground.

There was nothing to suggest that anything was amiss in the trees until they heard the sound of barking approaching.

From out of the darkness, Pattinson sprang towards the horses, causing them to spook a little. There was nowhere for them to bolt to and it took a few moments for the four men to steady their horses.

"Where the hell did that come from?" one of the riders gasped as he looked down at the dog and patted the neck of his horse soothingly.

"I am guessing from wherever it is we are going," Arwyn said with a wry smile.

Hunter dismounted and went to greet his dog with great affection.

"Where is she boy?" Alex whispered to his hound and the next moment he bounded away, back through the trees. Hunter followed the dog without a word, leading his horse behind him.

The dog raced back to the cave entrance that was not too far from where Pattinson had found his owner.

"I take it this is where we were headed, gentlemen?" Mr Hunter asked as he tired the reins of his horse to a tree.

"It is," one of them exclaimed with surprise.

"Very well, the three of you stay here and keep watch, in case our quarry is not within. I will be back shortly," Alex said as he whistled for Pattinson to follow him and ducked into the cave.

"I don't know, he started whining and then wrenched himself free and ran off!" Stanley Baker was whining to Lady Sarah as the groundskeeper entered the cave. He looked as white as a sheet and as though he was about to cry. Sylvia and Richard were exploring the back of the cave with Lee Baker and seemed unaware that anyone else was in the cave.

"I wouldn't worry about him," Alex announced himself with a note of amusement in his voice and Pattinson barked excitedly before rushing over to Lady Sarah, his tail wagging furiously as he did so.

"Mr Hunter, what a surprise," Lady Sarah said with a bemused look on her face.

"I take it that you have not found anything useful here?" Mr Hunter asked with a mild tone as he walked towards where Richard was.

"Nothing, I suspect this is a rarely used storeroom for some purpose, not anything more," Richard said with a sigh.

"It would be somewhat cramped if anyone were to live in this place for any length of time," Alex agreed.

"And what brings you here, Mr Hunter? I understood that you and the constable were to scout ahead and see what signs you could find of my lady's missing friends," Sylvia asked with a thinly veiled level of contempt for the man.

She was not well disposed towards any man that would impregnate a woman and then abandon her, let alone a man that would abandon her once she had lost the child.

There was very little in this world that would ever

convince her that he was a worthy man or a man that should be given the smallest amount of consideration.

"This is the location that Edryd discovered, according to the riders, but alas there is no one here," Alex shrugged and glared at the lady's maid.

"But they have to be somewhere close, we came all this way to find them," Lee Baker said stubbornly and looked at the four adults in turn.

The logic of children, though often flawed was nigh on impossible to refute at times.

"We will find them, Lee, do not worry. No attempt to find them is ever a waste," Lady Sarah said soothingly as she beckoned the boy over and held him tightly.

"Where are Arwyn and his father's men?" Richard asked Alex, trying to dispel the uncomfortable atmosphere that had settled in the cave.

"They are standing watch outside," Alex replied, "Where are your father, Miss DeVille, Derwyn, and Gordon?" he asked in return.

"They are at the Fox and Grapes in Hawarden, along with Edward and Thomas Egerton and their American cousin," Richard replied trying his best to suppress a laugh as he watched Hunter's face sour at the mention of his new rival for the affections of Lady Sarah.

"We should go back there and let them know what we have discovered and discredit the myth of highwaymen in the area with the landlord," Sylvia said firmly.

Lady Sarah opened her mouth to agree, but Pattinson began to growl and cut her off.

"What is it?" the young lady frowned at the dog.

"Wait here," Alex said firmly and motioned for Richard to follow him.

The two men strode quickly across the cave and ducked out of the entrance. Pattinson sat beside Lady Sarah, his fur bristling and the low growl stuck in his throat.

Lee and Stanley stood in front of Lady Sarah, ready to fight for her should the need arise.

Sylvia continued to rummage through the containers of supplies, trying to find anything that seemed out of place or might give a clue to the identity of those that used the cave.

Mr Hunter and Richard scrambled out of the cave and looked around them, nothing seemed amiss, but the dog had not started growling without cause.

"What has you looking so worried?" Arwyn frowned at the sudden appearance of the two men.

"Something or someone is coming," Mr Hunter replied and anxiously scanned the treeline.

They waited for a number of minutes but the night was still and there was no sign of anyone coming.

"We should go back and tell the ladies that all is well. It is time we left here anyway," Richard said.

He went back through the mouth of the cave and reappeared almost instant;y.

"Hunter, Arwyn, come quickly," he sounded breathless and worried and disappeared back inside the cave.

Neither Arwyn nor Mr Hunter dithered but immediately dashed after Richard Hales.

As they entered the gloom of the cavern, they saw a sight of destruction. Lee and Stanley Baker were stood at the back of the cave behind Lady Sarah and Sylvia.

Sylvia held one of the barrel lids in her hand and blood was smeared over it.

Pattinson was growling, his sharp teeth on show and drool falling from his mouth.

Lady Sarah stood with one hand on the neck of the dog whilst the other held her pistol which was pointed at two men who had pressed themselves against the wall of the cave.

One of the men was clutching his arm whilst the other clutched his nose.

"I will go fetch my father and your brother," Richard said to Arwyn and disappeared once more.

"What happened?" Mr Hunter asked with astonishment.

"The cave over there, there is an entrance you cannot see unless you are right on top of it," Sylvia said, pointing in a vague direction, but not taking her eyes off the two men.

"These men came from deeper within. They were waiting for you to leave and planned to add us to their captives it seems," Lady Sarah said with a calm voice that did nothing to reassure the men staring at her pistol.

"When they attacked, they did not expect the Baker boys to be such terriers, or that Pattinson would be so quick to try and deprive one of them of their limbs," Sylvia flashed a nasty smile at the two men.

"There is another entrance to the cave it seems, one

that allows smugglers to escape when authorities come in search of them. They came back and upon hearing voices came to investigate," Lady Sarah explained.

"Which is why Pattinson began growling," Mr Hunter nodded.

"Quite, but when you understandably went outside, they decided to attack and found the Sylvia was very handy with using a barrel lid as both a shield and sword," Lady Sarah said with a small amount of satisfaction.

"And that well-born ladies are not all helpless creatures and that when one of them threatens you with a gun it is more than a little terrifying?" Mr Hunter laughed.

"Who are they?" Arwyn asked, more concerned with who the men were than how they came to be captured.

"We have yet to discover that, but I feel that our friends could be persuaded to provide us with some information," Sylvia said with a menacing glint in her eye.

"Keep these crazy women away from us," one of the men stuttered.

"Perhaps, but first we want to know why you are here. Whom are you working for and what have you been doing in this cave?" Hunter asked.

The two men refused to reply and continued to look uneasily at Lady Sarah and Sylvia.

"If you decide to help us, we'll let you go home to your families after you've returned what you stole. Otherwise, we will have no choice but to take you over the border to the jail in Chester," Arwyn said firmly to the two men.

One of them sneered but neither of them volunteered any further reaction or information.

"Are you waiting for someone to come and rescue you?" Lady Sarah asked with a deadpan expression.

Neither man answered her.

"We have eaten and rested, we have nowhere we must be. We can wait all night," Sylvia warned the two men. There was something akin to fear that flittered briefly across the faces of the two men, but it was gone as quickly as it had appeared.

Arwyn glanced at Hunter, who shrugged. Neither man was adept at talking or extracting information without the help of outside influences. So they stood in silence. Waiting for inspiration to strike.

The sounds of scrambling and general noise

heralded the arrival of Richard with the others.

"Well, well it looks like we missed all of the fun!" Gordon said clapping his hands as he took stock of the situation in the cave.

"It is something of a rather dreary bore now," Lady Sarah sighed.

"Are these gentlemen going to stand there all night?" the doctor asked with a frown.

"That depends on their attitudes. They have been offered an incentive to help us, but they refuse to even open their mouths. We shall just have to take them back to Chester and let the police deal with them," Sarah replied with a shrug.

"What if we offer them something else first?" Derwyn suggested and talked to his brother in a low voice for a moment or two.

Once he had finished, Arwyn nodded in agreement, and Derwyn walked over to where the two men stood, looking even more nervous than before.

"Tell them what they want to know, and you can come and work for my family on our farm. It's not far down the road. You'll have a home, hot meals and money. It's hard work but you'll get respect if you do your best. You've also got protection from whomever it is you're working for now. Otherwise, I'll let my brother take you off to Chester and let the police get the information they are after our of those thick skulls," Derwyn gave the two men a wry smile and then sat down on the floor to await an answer.

He had barely brushed the floor with his behind when one of the men chirped,

"All right, we'll tell you. But you got to promise you'll do everything you said," he said earnestly to Derwyn.

"You have my word," Derwyn promised.

"We were here, all of us for a few months. There are a lot of caves and there was enough space for us. We came here last year. We'd been given a job to kidnap a woman but we didn't know which one it was we were supposed to take, so we took them both. We had them both here but we kept them separate so they couldn't try to escape or nothing," the first man began.

"The boss arranged for them to be moved to a house after a few months when they were sure no one was following them. We thought we were going out of the country, but after the ships stopped sailing, the plan changed and we had to wait here longer. The guy who talks to the boss, he's getting all tight and twisted about having to stay here and not going to America," the second man stuttered as he looked over all the faces of the group as they listened to him without comment.

"Do you know where this house is?" Lady Sarah asked as she lowered her gun, but did not call off Pattinson.

"No, they didn't tell us. We had to stay here and guard the supplies. They don't want anyone going into the villages if it can be avoided, so the boss gets supplies sent here to us. We just stay here or go to the pub. The others come at the same time every week to get some supplies and then go off again," the first man replied.

"You go to the pub? But aren't you supposed to stay out of the villages?" the doctor frowned.

"We've been here too long to worry about that now. We waited until all the farms had their extra hands coming in to help with harvests before we started going there, but since then, everyone knows who we are. We saw you at the pub tonight, but didn't think you'd be the ones to come snooping here," the second man said with a dry smile and a shake of his head.

"Have you been expecting someone to come?" Richard asked.

"We've been expecting the constables to come looking, but none of them has been out this way for a long time. That one's the first I've seen since we left England," the first man said as he nodded in Arwyn's direction.

"Always happy to see the police then?" Arwyn snorted.

"How did you know we were here?" the second man asked.

"We've had people looking all over the British Isles for the two women you had here, it was only a matter of time before we found you," Gordon said testily.

"About this house, you have no idea where it is?" Sylvia asked as she directed the conversation back to the point.

"No, we don't," the first man bristled at the tone in Sylvia's voice.

"You haven't heard a place mentioned or a direction that the supplies were taken in?" Lady Sarah asked in a much calmer tone than Sylvia used.

"Now that you mention it, I have heard them

mention Ashdown. It was a village that belonged to an Englishman's house with the same name. It's to the north, near the border, and it's roughly the same direction the supplies get taken in," the second man said thoughtfully.

"Is Ashdown empty now?" Edward asked with curiosity.

"It should be; it fell down in a storm a few years ago. Killed the man who owned it. He didn't have any family or friends, so it's been lying as a pile of rubble for years now. People swear it's haunted and don't go near the place," the first man shrugged.

"Very well, it is late now. We should head to bed before we go to Ashdown in the morning. We should send the riders back to the farm, we don't need them to come with us. Perhaps they will be glad to take our new friends here to the farm and introduce them to your father," the doctor said, bringing the questions to a close.

"I'll write a letter to my father, he'll not know what to think otherwise," Derwyn sighed and searched through the cave until he found a scrap of paper and used a piece of charcoal from the dead fire to scrawl a quick note to his father.

He paused and thought for a few moments about how best to phrase things and how much of an explanation he should give. In the end, he decided to be brief so it simply read:

Two men farmhands. Get them set. Will explain later.

Derwyn

Chapter 11

The two riders agreed to take the two turncoats back to the farm with them, accompanied by the letter from Derwyn. Arwyn made sure to take the riders aside and impress upon the two men that they weren't to be trusted until they proved otherwise.

The party watched the four men disappearing down the road on the four horses from the farm before they turned and made their way back to Hawarden.

The landlord of the Fox and Grapes was only too happy to provide another room for his guests, as well as food and drink for Mr Hunter and Constable Evans.

Lady Sarah excused herself almost as soon as they arrived back at the inn, and made her way to bed with Pattinson following her closely.

The doctor followed her example soon after, wanting to not only get his bones to bed, but he also wanted to make sure that the two Baker boys got enough sleep. He had a feeling that no matter where the search for Millie and Grace led, they would all need to be as sharp as possible.

Oliver excused himself alongside the doctor, which also prompted Derwyn and Miss DeVille to say their goodnights to their companions. Derwyn walked Oliver to his room with a friendly arm around his shoulders whilst Miss DeVille went quietly to her bed in the shared room with Lady Sarah.

Richard went to check on the horses and the coachmen before he too made for his bed. The coachmen had elected to sleep in the groom's quarters, which was closer to the horses, just in case anything happened during the night.

This left Alex and Arwyn to eat their meals in the company of Edward, Thomas, Gordon and Sylvia. The Egerton brothers talked of trivial things and tried to give the impression that they were merely a large party travelling to visit friends in the country.

Alex and Arwyn were silent, listening to the brothers as they ate, but both thinking over what they had learned in the cave.

It was strange to them both that there was a

nameless boss behind everything. It begged the questions as to whether Lady de Mandeville was behind the kidnapping or whether someone else was involved. The infamous lady never used her own name in her more suspect dealings, reverting to the moniker of John Smith, so why would it be that the nondescript alias was being hidden from these men.

It didn't make sense to either man, but neither had reached enough of a conclusion to speak of it to anyone else.

Sylvia sat and observed Mr Hunter with a steely glare. She was almost certain that he could not be trusted, but she would not stop watching him until she was absolutely positive that his influence should be kept away from her mistress.

There was very little that he did that she did not see, and the intensity that she viewed him with was not lost on the groundskeeper. He knew that he had a near-impossible task to convince both Lady Sarah and her maid that he was worthy of the lady's hand.

Gordon listened to the two Egerton men talk, his teeth grinding more and more as they continued to drone on about nothing even close to being interesting or connected to the one thing that was in the forefront of his mind.

His jaw continued to tighten until he could not contain himself any longer, and he slammed his fists down on the table, causing Arwyn and Alex's drinks to fall over, spilling beer across the table.

"Easy there, old chap," Edward said as he pushed his chair back from the table to avoid the spill of alcohol.

"Easy? We are all taking things far too calmly and sedately, and you tell me to be easy?" Gordon growled as he narrowed his eyes at Edward.

"We know you want to find Millie as soon as we can, but come now, it is hardly worth spilling beer over," Thomas tried to calm Gordon down but his platitudes only served to make the doctor's son angrier.

"How could you know what this feels like to know whether it is worth spilling beer over? Not one of you has ever had someone you love taken from you with no warning and left no trace behind to follow. You cannot possibly fathom how it feels to have suddenly a shred of hope that you might be finally able to find her, to be reunited with her, only for your companions to trundle through it all as though there was all the time in the world,"

Gordon sneered and scowled at each of the four men in turn.

"What a child you are," Sylvia spat from beside Thomas.

The four men all turned surprised eyes on the lady's maid.

"Excuse me?" Gordon snarled.

"You may very well beg to be excused, but your behaviour is quite inexcusable," Sylvia replied shortly.

Gordon didn't know what to say in reply and blinked at her several times as he struggled to find the words in his mind.

"All these people have come all this way, have been searching and risking so much to find these two women, and you, when this close to finding them, are now throwing this tantrum. You're a childish fool and do not deserve the consideration and patience your friends have given you," Sylvia said as she gracefully rose to her feet.

"Gentlemen, enjoy the rest of your evening," she said to the others and turned away without another word.

"Now there is a good woman to help her ladyship stay out of trouble," Thomas smiled as he watched the woman walk away.

"She is certainly made of sterner stuff than most," Edward said with admiration.

"She needs to learn when to keep her opinions to herself," Gordon huffed.

"Perhaps, but there are those who would do well to keep their anger in check in front of her if they do not want to be lectured," Edward shrugged.

Arwyn and Mr Hunter kept their thoughts about Sylvia to themselves. Arwyn liked the woman, but she did have a tendency to speak out of turn.

Mr Hunter did not like the woman. He did not like the way she looked at him or the way she distrusted him. Though the distrust and dislike had been thoroughly earned, it did not stop him from resenting her for it.

The five men did not spend much longer in the tavern after Sylvia departed. They filtered off to bed one after another. Mr Hunter was the last to turn in. He waited in the tavern for an extra hour to watch the thinning crowd for any faces that had been a little too interested in their party.

Soon there was just a handful of men left drinking,

two men too drunk to lift their heads from the table, and three who were huddled together in a far corner.

Though the three huddled men looked suspicious, there was nothing to suggest to Mr Hunter that they had been paying any attention to anything other than whatever matter they had been discussing since he had arrived.

They had not looked up or away from each other for any length of time since Mr Hunter had sat down. The ingress and egress of patrons had no effect on the intensity of their conversation. Alex concluded that their purpose was not linked to his or that of his friends, but he made sure to make note of their faces, just in case he was wrong.

The following morning, the tavern was empty as the group made their way down to breakfast. They were the only guests in the inn that night, and the innkeeper was grateful to have rented so many rooms in a single night.

The horses had been well taken care of and the carriages were repacked quickly by the drivers. There was nothing that could be said to be wrong with the Fox and Grapes, but still, Arwyn was glad to be leaving it.

He had felt on edge since they had returned from the cave. There was nothing that he could put his finger on as to why he felt so uneasy, but he made sure that he was on his guard when the carriages were ready to pull out of the inn.

He sat up beside the driver and watched the road carefully for any signs of them being followed.

The carriages were becoming quite crowded, so much so that Sylvia, Miss DeVille and Lady Sarah all piled into her ladyship's carriage with Pattinson, Derwyn, Doctor Hales, Mr Hunter and the Baker Boys climbed into the carriage that had held Sylvia and Miss DeVille, and Richard, Gordon, Edward, Oliver and Thomas all squeezed into the largest carriage.

"We should have brought mother's spare carriage, we could have travelled in style," Thomas complained as he tried to pull his jacket pocket out from underneath his brother.

The drivers were given instruction to head towards the hamlet of Ashdown to continue their search. Derwyn was anxious to get home, but he knew that their purpose was not to bring him home to his mother and father with his fiance but to find the missing women.

His homecoming to a fatted calf would have to wait until they had finished following up on the information that the two bandits had provided.

The hamlet of Ashdown was not far from Hawarden, but it might as well have been a hundred miles for the differences that the group encountered there.

The hamlet was a small community that was formed around the ruins of the great house that had once stood at its centre. It looked to Lady Sarah as though the hamlet was mainly comprised of the cottages from the estate and a sprinkling of new homes that had been built from the rubble of the main house.

Some of the houses were well built, others seemed ready to collapse under the slightest gust of wind. The carriages pulled up at the edge of the hamlet and Pattinson jumped to his feet, barking with delight at being able to disembark so soon from his prison on wheels.

The drivers did not alight from their perches, and Miss DeVille and Sylvia elected to remain in their carriage whilst the others explored the area.

Pattinson rushed off the moment the carriage door opened and frolicked around in the long grass at the side of the narrow track that led into the hamlet.

Those that lived in the hamlet appeared to be

farmers, but they were local men and women that had never left the hamlet, save to take their wares to the market in Hawarden once a month.

To have three fancy carriages pull up on their doorstep, and to see such a collection of men and a grand lady with a terrifying dog emerge from inside was positively terrifying to the population there.

Three children had been playing in the dirt by the well when the carriages had arrived at the hamlet, but the moment the doors had opened, they had scurried inside the nearest hut and shut the door firmly behind them.

A woman hanging out clean laundry abandoned her basket and rushed away towards the fields.

"A warm welcome," Oliver said dryly as he looked around the hamlet with a look that could only be described as disgust.

"We are not in America or the great cities of England. People in the far reaches of the countryside are not used to visitors or know how to act around anyone other than those that they have spent their lives around," Mr Hunter replied flatly.

"Hello? We are not here to alarm or harm you!"

Lady Sarah called out, ignoring the petty squabble between the two men.

Nobody replied or appeared to greet the group.

"Wait here, it may need a more local touch," Derwyn winked at the lady and beckoned to his brother to follow him in the direction that the woman had run.

"Pattinson, stop being such a fool," Lady Sarah laughed as she watched the Akita trying to chase after three butterflies at once.

"Do you think that we will find any answers here?" Thomas asked the lady as he moved slowly over to stand beside her.

"No, but who knows? If you were trying to hide two kidnapped women, a remote place such as this would be the perfect place to hide away from those that were searching tirelessly for them," Lady Sarah shrugged.

"True, and the locals here do seem to be rather averse to visitors," Edward smiled.

"Fear and surprise are two different things," Oliver sighed as he leaned against the carriage.

"You think that it is surprise that caused the three children to run inside?" Mr Hunter asked with a bemused expression.

"No, I think being told to run inside whenever they see strangers is why they ran inside. The same thing that all children are taught," Mr Brown replied hotly.

"We were never taught to run away from strangers," Stanley said flatly.

"Your mother never told you to run away from strangers?" Oliver frowned at the twins.

"No, we see strangers all the time in the shop. Running away from them would be a pretty silly way to run a business," Lee replied with a straight face that even caused the doctor to smirk slightly.

"Come now, we could stand here and try to guess why the people here are so quick to flee from strangers, but until Arwyn and Derwyn have come back, there is no use arguing about it," the doctor said firmly as he recovered his composure.

"You are quite right, doctor, we should not be trying to guess. Stanley, Lee, see if you can get the children in the house to talk to you through the door," Lady Sarah said with a slight smile.

The two Baker boys grinned broadly and sprang

forward to do as Lady Sarah asked.

"Why the boys?" Oliver asked with interest.

"You might be right about the children being told to run from strangers, but children have this wonderful way of seeing all children as their friends the moment they meet them. There is no thought in their little innocent heads that there could be anything nefarious in the heart of another child. Only adults are to be mistrusted," Lady Sarah replied brightly.

"And with good reason," the doctor smiled.

"Quite, though we may well have seen more than our fair share of adults with poisoned hearts," Lady Sarah replied with a sigh.

"What is it?" Mr Hunter asked with concern, causing Lady Sarah to blush slightly.

"I was merely wondering what it is that causes hearts to become so terribly corrupt. Is it simply the way the world is? Cruelty to one another, or is it just that certain people are destined to become this way?" Lady Sarah asked no one in particular, but the questions were enough to plunge the men into deep thought.

"I am not sure you will ever know," Sylvia said as

she leant out of the carriage window, "But if we assume that kindness is enough to change the hate in this world, perhaps it is something we should all practice a little more of."

"You would have more experience than most of how kindness can change a heart," Mr Hunter said dryly.

"And you, sir, would have more of a notion as to the damage that cruelty can do," Sylvia replied with a wave of her hand and disappeared back inside the carriage.

"Perhaps the pair of you might have better luck talking to the children," the doctor said dryly as he fixedly stared at Mr Hunter with a raised eyebrow.

Lady Sarah made no comment, instead, she watched Lee and Stanley Baker approach the cottage that the children had disappeared inside of and knock on what passed for a door.

There was no doubt in her mind that if the two boys put their minds to it, they could easily break down the pieces of wood that covered the opening, but the Baker boys had more sense than to do that.

They sat down on either side of the door and knocked gently on it. They kept their voices kind and light and asked questions about favourite games. When they got no reply they talked to each other about their favourite games as children and how much they missed playing with other children.

They talked about pranks they played and the trouble they got into, but nothing elicited any response from those inside the house.

After fifteen minutes of trying, Lady Sarah motioned for the two boys to come back to her.

"We're sorry," they chorused.

"No boys, you did your best. I think we can safely assume now that fear is indeed their motivation for hiding," Lady Sarah said and chewed her bottom lip in thought.

"What is it that they would be so afraid of that they would go so far to hide from us?" Edward asked.

"I do not know, but I hope that Arwyn and Derwyn have more luck in their quest for answers. It is possible that the children cannot speak English and therefore they did not understand anything Lee and Stanley said. If that is the case, I can understand why they would not reply," Lady Sarah surmised.

"It is a possibility," Thomas agreed and sighed.

"It will take as long as it takes. I know that there is nowhere here to eat and we do not know how long it will be before we reach the Evans farm to eat. But please, be patient, it will not be too long," Lady Sarah begged Thomas in a low voice.

"My apologies, my lady, I did not mean to appear impatient. I know how important it is for us to discover all that we can here," Thomas replied with a slight bow.

"Would you object to us going after Arwyn and Derwyn to find out how they are progressing, or would you rather we stayed together?" Gordon asked with a slight scowl

"You are free to do as you see fit, but I would hope that you would not wander too far from us," the doctor said looking at his son with a mix of worry and frustration.

"Do not worry father, I will go with him and keep him from harming himself and others," Richard said in a low voice so that only the doctor would hear.

"Be careful," the doctor said warmly in reply.

The two brothers began to walk in the direction that Arwyn and Derwyn headed in but a few steps into the fields, they stopped and turned back.

"I suspect that Arwyn and Derwyn are coming back now," Edward observed.

"Should we go meet them?" Thomas asked.

"No, let us wait here, we are better to talk at the edge of the village than in the centre of it," Lady Sarah replied.

It did not take long for the four men to return to their waiting friends.

"What did you discover?" Mr Hunter asked as Arwyn and Derwyn returned.

"The people here do not speak English, but they are not willing to talk to us in Welsh either. Something or someone has clearly terrified them. They kept telling us to go or more would be lost," Derwyn sighed and ran his fingers through his hair.

"What will be lost?" Richard frowned.

"They would not say anything else," Arwyn replied and shook his head.

"Something terrible is happening here, it seems too much of a coincidence to be unconnected. The bandits sent us here after all," the doctor mused.

"Perhaps we should leave here, for now, the hamlet

will not disappear. We should go to the farm, eat a good meal and try to fit the small pieces of what we know together. After all, the farmhands, the bandits or Edryd may know more that can help us," Edward said clapping his hands together.

"Very well, I will go fetch Pattinson and we shall depart," Lady Sarah agreed. Since they had arrived Pattinson had run off around the village chasing butterflies, but since Derwyn and Arwyn had returned, no one had kept watch over the dog.

"You shouldn't go alone," Sylvia said as she opened the carriage and climbed out.

"We'll come too," Lee volunteered, cutting off any others who might have wished to accompany the two ladies.

"Very well, we shall not be long," Lady Sarah smiled and she, the Baker boys, and Sylvia went off in the direction they had last seen Pattinson go, calling out his name as they went.

Chapter 12

"Pattinson, come here!" Lady Sarah called out, as she, Stanley and Lee Baker, and Sylvia made their way around the edge of the hamlet in search of the dog.

"Where can he have gotten to?" Sylvia frowned as she looked about for the dog.

"There's a lot of houses here, he could have gone inside one of them," Lee suggested.

"How would he get through the doors?" Stanley asked with exasperation.

"There are a lot of houses here. But there are not many children," Lady Sarah said slowly.

"What do you mean?" Sylvia frowned.

"For a place with so many homes, so many people working the land, there should be more children. There were three outside when we arrived, but they ran inside and when they refused to come out - we must find Pattinson quickly and rejoin the others," Lady Sarah said with a sudden and horrific realisation.

Lee and Stanley ran ahead of the two ladies and soon found Pattinson stalking birds through the long grass.

He was reluctant to return to the carriage, but at the urging of Lady Sarah, the dog padded his way obediently back at her side.

The others were already in their carriages waiting to depart when they returned. Lady Sarah's face was white with worry and her eyes were pricked with tears.

"Your ladyship, what is wrong?" Miss DeVille asked as she climbed into the carriage.

"She will tell us when we arrive at the farm. Let her think in silence for a while," Sylvia said as she climbed up behind Lady Sarah. Pattinson was the last to jump into the carriage and settled himself beside Lady Sarah, lying with his head in her lap.

She absentmindedly stroked his head whilst the carriage lurched along the road and out of the hamlet. The young lady had no concept of time passing as the Welsh countryside went by.

Sylvia and Miss DeVille sat in silence and looked out of the carriage windows. Sylvia wondered about what was going through Lady Sarah's mind but felt it was best to wait until she was ready to speak.

Miss DeVille resented the way Sylvia spoke to her and so she thought ugly thoughts about the woman who sat beside her and fed her own hatred with unworthy thoughts.

Lady Sarah didn't know how long she had been in the carriage for certain but it seemed like mere minutes had passed when the carriage stopped and the door opened.

"We are here, my lady," the driver said as he extended his hand and offered to help her down. Pattinson pushed to be the first out of the carriage but Sylvia held him firmly by his collar and made him wait until the humans had all disembarked.

"It is rather quiet," Derwyn frowned as he looked around the familiar farmyard.

Arwyn stood drinking in his surroundings as it was the first time he was back at the farm since he had run away to Stickleback Hollow. It felt strange to him to have come so far in his own life to be returning to a life he had resisted for so long.

It was not as though he was returning to a prison he had thrown off but a familiar place he could not look back at fondly, knowing he did not belong but would be lingering there only for a short time.

Most of all he was looking forward to seeing his mother. Though she was a hard woman, she was also loving and warm as a mother. She had spent hours encouraging Arwyn when he was a boy and educating him when the duties of farm life meant that going to school was impossible.

As a farmer's son, he was not poor but he was by no means the son of a gentleman, so his education had always been a secondary consideration. But he could read and write well enough and he had excellent skills of logic that his mother had helped him to develop over the years.

He had not even noticed the lack of activity on the farm until his brother had mentioned it.

"That is odd, I did not notice it when we came to change horses. But we were here for so short a time and I was so focused on the journey, not the farm," Arwyn said shaking his head.

"Wait here, I am going to see who I can find to tell us what has happened here," Derwyn said and walked off in the direction of the fields.

"Perhaps we can go inside? I think her ladyship needs to sit down," the doctor suggested as he eyed Lady Sarah with concern.

"Please doctor, I am al right, it is just a thought that occurred to me whilst we were searching for Pattinson," Lady Sarah said with a wave of her hand.

"What is that?" Oliver asked with curiosity.

"There were not enough children there. For the number of homes and people, there were only three children. Three children who ran and hid, not making a sound when entreated to come out," Lady Sarah explained with a deep sadness in her voice.

"My God," Mr Hunter said as he ran his hand through his hair and contemplated the implications of Lady Sarah's thoughts.

"What? What do you think such a thing means?" Oliver asked with a frown.

"That someone is taking the children from their homes. The reason that no one would speak to us, it all comes back to their children," the doctor sighed and shook his head with disgust.

"Then we need to talk to our bandit friends about

the kidnapping of children as well as Grace and Millie," Thomas said, barely controlling the anger in his voice.

"Misters Egerton, perhaps, you, Mr Hunter and Mr Brown could come with me to locate the men in question and we can allow the ladies and the doctor to go inside and wait for us all in the living room. Please, doctor, knock, I am sure my mother will be glad to see you," Arwyn said and led the men away with him.

"What are we supposed to do?" Richard laughed, as he, Gordon, and the Baker boys looked between the two groups.

"Unpack the carriage and help the drivers see to the horses, I am sure that it is not beyond your many skills to do so," the doctor teased his son.

"Ah, I see, fit only to fetch and carry, it is like the summers we used to spend here as boys," Richard laughed and nudged his brother in the ribs with his elbow.

"Those times seem so far away now," Gordon could not help but smile.

"Come, Lee, Stanley, we have been given a task and we must do it with all the vigour we can muster!" Richard exclaimed and left Jack Hales to lead the three women to the door of the farmhouse.

He knocked on the door quite firmly and waited. There was no answer, so he knocked again.

It took three rounds of knocking before the door was opened, but not by Bronwyn Evans, instead, it was Edryd that stood in the doorway.

His skin was sallow and his eyes were bloodshot.

"Dear Lord, Edryd, what on earth has happened!" Doctor Hales exclaimed as he beheld the shadow of his friend.

"I will go fetch the others, " Sylvia said without a moment's hesitation and took off at a run across the yard, her skirts lifted up so she would not trip as she ran.

The doctor took Edryd by the arm and walked him into the house. He sat him in a kitchen chair and Miss DeVille busied herself with making a pot of tea.

Lady Sarah and Pattinson followed behind the doctor and farmer and sat beside him at the table.

"You must tell us what has happened, there are so many questions we have for you, but we cannot ask you them in this state, so first we must know your troubles," the doctor said gently as he held Edryd's wrist and took his pulse.

"Ever the practising physician," Edryd smiled weakly at the doctor, who frowned and sighed in reply.

"Where is your wife?" Lady Sarah asked, "I was so looking forward to meeting her."

At the mention of Bronwyn, whatever colour remained in the farmer's face vanished.

"She is not well," Edryd said stiltedly.

"Ah well, then it is a good thing there is a doctor here," the doctor said brightly and moved away from Edryd towards the staircase in the corridor.

"Wait, Jack, don't," Edryd said, suddenly leaping to his feet.

"And why should I not attend a patient?" the doctor asked with a stony expression on his face.

"She was seen by a doctor, she just needs rest," Edryd stuttered.

"Tush and nonsense," Jack Hales dismissed his friend's protests and started up the stairs.

"Please, don't," Edryd begged and made to stop the doctor but Pattinson was on his feet and barred the way with a flash of his teeth and a low growl.

"Do you want to tell me the truth before I discover it for myself?" the doctor asked from the stairs.

"I am telling you the truth," Edryd protested.

"Very well, we shall soon see," the doctor replied and carried on his way.

It was not his first time visiting the house and he knew the way to Bronwyn and Edryd's bedroom without having to be told where to go. If Bronwyn was truly ill, then the only logical place for her to be found was in her bed.

The doctor felt apprehensive as he made his way down the landing corridor towards the bedroom door. Edryd's protests and strange behaviour had him worried.

He paused outside of the bedroom and took a deep breath. He could hear animated voices coming from below and was certain that Sylvia had brought at least some of the men back to the house.

The doctor turned the handle and pushed the door open. The bedroom was as it should be, all except for Bronwyn. She was lying in bed, her fall swollen, her lips cut and her chest barely moving.

Doctor Jack Hales had seen his fair share of beaten men in his time. He had seen the terrible things that men do to one another on the battlefield and the injuries that bayonets and bullets could do to the human body.

The state that Bronwyn had been left in shocked even him.

He had known this woman for many years and had never thought that he would see her in such a broken and battered condition. He moved quietly about the room and began to examine her, but not without first telling her what he was doing.

Jack spoke in his most gentle voice to put her as much at ease as he could. It was half an hour before he finished his examination and was about to return to the kitchen, only to find both Arwyn and Derwyn rushing into the room.

The two men were rocked by quick-shifting emotions as they beheld their vulnerable mother. First came shock, then anger, grief, denial, and a bitter desire for revenge.

"How is she?" Arwyn asked the doctor in a hushed voice.

"She will live. As to how she is, that is something we will not know for quite some time. Come, it is best to let her rest. Tell her you love her and make the promises you need to, then join me downstairs," the doctor said kindly and left the Evans brothers alone with their mother.

Derwyn and Arwyn watched the doctor leave and shut the door behind him.

"Mother, we finally drag Arwyn home and this happens, the trouble you manage to get into," Derwyn said lovingly as he stroked his mother's hair.

Bronwyn's eyes flickered and discernible sounds passed her lips, but what words they were was anybody's guess.

Arwyn took his mother's hand gently and smiled at her.

"We're both here and whoever did this will be made to pay, mother, you just rest and know that we love you," the policeman said with affection.

The two men did not linger long in their mother's room and returned promptly to the kitchen as the doctor had ordered.

Their father was sat in the kitchen with Miss DeVille beside him. The doctor had his stethoscope on and was listening to Edryd's chest.

The farmer had protested at first but had seemingly lost his will to fight, and had soon relented to the doctor's need to perform his medical duties.

"Where is everyone else?" Arwyn asked as he looked around the deserted kitchen.

"They are in the front room. They wanted to discuss events whilst I focused my attention on this foolish patient," the doctor replied with a slight tone of annoyance in his voice.

"That is for the best then, we wanted to talk to our father without the others here," Derwyn said with a stony face.

"I have nothing to say," Edryd sighed.

"That will change," Derwyn growled in reply. Arwyn placed his hand on his brother's arm to calm him.

"Father, what happened here?" Arwyn asked gently.

"Nothing," Edryd said shortly.

"Then you did that to mother?" Derwyn asked with exasperation. He knew his father had never raised a hand to his mother, and never would.

"Don't be so stupid," Edryd chided his son.

"Then what happened?" Arwyn asked crossly.

"Nothing that concerns you," Edryd replied.

"You believe that to be true? That the assault on our mother is no concern of ours?" Derwyn asked angrily.

Edryd did not reply but instead stared straight ahead.

"The stubbornness of an old Welshman is not to be underestimated. Perhaps you should go to Lady Sarah and talk to her about your mother," the doctor said tilting his head towards the door and gesturing with it that the two men should leave.

"Miss DeVille, perhaps you would be good enough to go too?" the doctor asked with a smile.

Miss DeVille nodded and stood quickly so she could take Derwyn's arm as the three left the room.

"I'm surprised at you," Jack Hales said when he was sure the others were all out of earshot. Edryd looked up at his friend with a weary expression on his face but showed no signs of shame or confessing to the doctor.

"Take this motley band of children off my farm and go home," Edryd sighed and tried to stand but the firm hand of the doctor pushed him down into his chair and held him there.

"You are going to sit there and listen," the doctor ordered, his voice raised but not quite a shout.

"You do not give the orders in my home," Edryd replied as he struggled to try and free himself from the doctor's grip.

"I am a doctor and given that your wife has been brutally attacked, I could have you committed as a violent man. You will not give any information to the police or your sons about what happened here, and so the conclusion of anyone who does not know you would be that you are the one responsible and should be locked away for the benefit of society. We both know that is not what you want, so you will sit here and you will listen to me. Then, you will go through and tell those children exactly what happened and they will help you. Once they are finished with you, you will go and sit by your wife's side with a shotgun to protect her from anyone that would harm her," the doctor growled.

Edryd stopped fighting and sat still in his chair. He nodded his head in agreement and the doctor took his hand off of the farmer's shoulder.

"What I believe, and I have no doubt Lady Sarah believes, happened is that someone amongst your farmhands is working for the villains that we have been searching for. That the moment you sent the poor Kveitus to Stickleback Hollow with your message, this individual informed those he truly works for of what you were doing, and they then informed men that were looking for him and had him killed to stop him from delivering your message. With that threat dealt with, they did not expect you to send another man, let alone two to deliver a new message. Unable to stop these messengers, the men came into your house and assaulted your wife to threaten you. I expect they scribbled something trite on your wall about compliance and keeping your mouth shut. So out of fear, you are now sitting with your lips sealed and you are willing to let down not only your friends but your wife and sons," the doctor sighed and shook his head as he sat down beside Edryd.

"And what would you have me do?" Edryd asked slowly as he turned to look at his old friend.

"I would have you find that spirit of the Valleys that you keep telling me about. The fight and steadfast dependability that your sons both believe you are made of. I would have you go tell those children everything, confirm suspicions, find the mole amongst your farmhands and do to him what was done to your wife. I would have you answer any questions that these children have, and then I would have you do everything to protect your wife and make your family proud," the doctor said with passion and leaned back in the kitchen chair.

"When you speak it sounds so simple," Edryd laughed to himself.

"The choices are simple, it is only the execution of them that is hard," the doctor said with a wry smile.

"Indeed, I doubt that I will ever forgive myself if I do not agree with you," Edryd sighed, "And I am not proud of myself for how I have been acting, but it does not mean it is easy to do."

"Come, we should go to the children now. We are wasting precious time," the doctor said and the two men rose from the table and went to find the others.

Chapter 13

Edryd was sheepish as he explained what had happened to his wife and the events that had led up to the attack. The group of visitors all listened quietly to him and waited until he was finished before they asked any questions.

"Then there is a traitor amongst our own people," Derwyn growled and clenched his fists.

"That would seem to be the case, but I do not know who," Edyrd shrugged.

"We will find out who it is, and they will be made to pay for their treachery," Arwyn said forcefully.

"Perhaps we should not spring to violence quite so quickly," Mr Brown cautioned and received reproachful looks from all three Evans men.

"I think Mr Brown is right. We may be able to use the traitor far more effectively to provide us with information rather than simply have us meeting out vengeance against his flesh," Lady Sarah said thoughtfully.

"But how would we find such a traitor?" Richard Hales asked with a frown.

"We set a trap for him, just as you might if you were hunting in a forest," Mr Hunter replied.

"To set a trap, you need bait," Mr Brown replied pointedly.

"Perhaps it would be better if we did not focus on the traitor, for now, we have more important things to deal with first," Edward replied tactfully.

"You think there is something more important than finding the man who sold his soul to evil men and harmed our mother?" Derwyn asked with narrowed eyes.

"I think discovering what happened to the children of Ashdown and looking for Grace and Millie should be our first priority," Thomas argued.

"And in the meantime we allow a traitor to stay here at the farm and risk the lives of everyone here?" Arwyn asked with disbelief.

"Peace, gentlemen, please," Lady Sarah begged as she held her hands up to silence the men and try to calm the tension that was building in the room.

"Arguing will get us nowhere, but I do not think the farm should be left unattended. Perhaps we should divide our resources to use them effectively," Gordon suggested thoughtfully.

"What do you suggest?" Sylvia asked.

"The doctor and ladies should stay here, Lady Sarah, Sylvia and the doctor should care for Bronwyn and watch over Edryd. Derwyn can take over running the farm and Miss DeVille can take on the duties that Bronwyn would ordinarily take care of. Mr Hunter and I should take some men and the bandits and explore the area to look for signs of anything strange, the bandits certainly know more than they have told us, but we can use their knowledge to search," Gordon replied.

"To look for the children or Grace and Millie?" Oliver asked.

"Both," Gordon said quickly.

"What will the rest of us do?" Richard asked with a raised eyebrow.

"Arwyn and the Baker boys can talk to the rest of the farmhands under the guise of work and gather information to try and find the traitor amongst the men here," Gordon suggested.

"And those of us that were not raised to work the land?" Edward asked hopefully.

"The four of you will stand guard around the house with Pattinson, make sure that no one comes into the house outside of those of us in this room, and my father. Edryd and Bronwyn are to remain in the house to keep them safe," Gordon replied.

Sylvia looked at the man with interest. He had seemingly taken all of his anger from the other night and transformed it into a singular focus. It was impressive, but Sylvia also knew how dangerous it was to bottle up emotions, especially rage that would build and could erupt at any time without warning.

"That does seem like the best course of action for now. Mr Evans, can you accompany Miss DeVille and myself to the kitchen so that the doctor and your father can be informed and we can be instructed as to Bronwyn's care and duties respectively," Sylvia's tone conveyed that she was not asking a question, but issuing an instruction to Derwyn and Miss DeVille.

Richard marvelled at the woman and her ability to

command obedience with a simple statement, how she was willing to stand up to others with no regard for rank or privilege. Sylvia was a woman who a strong mind and stronger convictions. Even in the face of those that would consider themselves her betters, she was able to speak with authority and find at least some who would listen.

He thought about the women in his society, the poise and freedom of spirit that Lady Sarah possessed that was so threatening to men like Captain Jonnes Smith; the quiet influence that Mrs Bosworth exerted over everyone, even the brigadier; the bustle and motherly heart of Cooky who did not care where someone was born and would reach out in friendship and love to them; the stoic strength of Lady Szonja that had withstood tragedy and the confines of the world she had been born into and forged a force that could stand firm in the face of any adversity; and now that of Sylvia.

He wondered about the new queen on her throne and how she would be transformed by her duties and how this would shape not only those of her subjects in England but the very face of the world. Richard did not have long to languor with these thoughts as Sylvia had turned her attention to him.

"I would suggest that the constable should show you any points of ingress and egress around the house that could be used to gain entry and whilst Mr Hales is taken on such a tour, the gentlemen of Tatton Park could think of how they plan to subdue and detain any one would-be attackers," Sylvia said with the same air of authority that caused all four men to nod.

"Come, Sylvia, you and I must discover how best to care for Bronwyn. We should talk to the doctor first, then Edryd," Lady Sarah said warmly as she summoned her companion to her side.

Pattinson leapt to his feet and made to go with his mistress.

"No Pattinson, you are to stay with Richard. He will need your help," Lady Sarah scratched the hunting dog between the ears as she spoke to him and sent him to sit at the feet of Richard. He waged his tail and barked understanding to his mistress and something told Richard that the dog knew that he was protecting his mistress more by his side than if the dog was with her.

Edward, Thomas and Oliver lapsed into

conversation whilst Arwyn lead Richard and Pattinson on a tour of the house, both inside and out, and though Richard had visited the farm as a child, much had changed and some things he had forgotten about the old house.

Once Richard was sure he knew of all the places that needed to be guarded, barricaded, or simply blocked off, he returned to the house to report to the men of Tatton Park. Pattinson sat outside the door to the kitchen and watched for even the slightest movement, his senses on high alert as he proudly guarded all those inside.

The Baker boys had waited patiently for Arwyn before they went to the fields to begin the hardest work they would ever undertake. Though young and fit, neither Lee nor Stanley had ever farmed before and they were unprepared for how gruelling the work would be.

Mr Hunter and Gordon made their way to the stables to saddle the horses before they fetched the men that would accompany them on their expedition.

Lady Sarah watched Mr Hunter working from Bronwyn's window and felt a pang in her chest over all that had been lost between them.

She could not help but love him still, even after

everything that had passed between them, but it did not mean she would readily trust him with her heart again.

She watched as the men assembled and mounted and rode out of the farmyard, her eyes fixed upon Alex until the last moment that he rode out of view.

Alex could feel that he was being watched as he worked tacking the horses. It was an instinct that served him well and had been developed by all his time working outside and away from people.

He did not dare to look for the source of the eyes whilst he focused on the task in front of him. He did not want the eyes to belong to anyone but Lady Sarah, and he could not be certain that they did until he looked.

Mr Hunter waited until the last possible moment to raise his gaze to the farmhouse. He was mounted upon Black Guy, Lady Sarah's horse, and relief flooded his body as he saw her watching him from the upper window.

He did not have long to enjoy the feeling of relief and hope that his gaze gave him, as Gordon, mounted upon Harald, was quick to move the group out of the farmyard.

He felt her eyes upon him as they left and the moment they were out of view of the house, he missed her and knew that he would do all that he could to find Grace and Millie to bring them home to her, not just for their sake, but his own.

To rebuild the trust he had broken, required a demonstration of devotion that could not be matched. To rescue two women that meant so much to the love of his life seemed like just the demonstration he required.

Lady Sarah sighed to herself as she watched the men leave and tried to bring her mind back to the duties she had to perform for Bronwyn. The doctor and Edryd were busy giving Sylvia detailed instructions on her care, and Lady Sarah had elected to go to Bronwyn to keep the woman company whilst the details were provided.

The door to the room opened and closed quietly. Lady Sarah turned, expecting to see Sylvia, but instead Mr Oliver Henry Brown stood in the room, smiling at her with a lopsided grin.

"You certainly have interesting adventures!" the American drawled at the young lady.

"Exciting even to one from America?" Lady Sarah asked with a coy smile.

"Of course, the wild untamed lands of the colonies

can't compare with the intrigue and danger that the motherland seems to hold," Oliver laughed and ran his hand through his hair.

"Did you require something particular or are you merely making sure that the room is secure?" Lady Sarah teased as she leaned against the wall.

"I am ensuring all is safe and well up here, but there is something, in particular, I do want," Mr Brown said and slowly walked over to where Lady Sarah stood.

"You should know that it is not proper for a man to be so close to a single young lady behind a closed door," Lady Sarah replied with a glint in her eye.

"But, my lady, Bronwyn is here, how could it be inappropriate?" Mr Brown replied with a wide grin. He gently took her hand in his and pressed his lips to it.

Lady Sarah blushed but did not withdraw her hand.

"My lady, you are the most intriguing woman I have ever met, and whilst we are alone, I would like to take the opportunity to -" Oliver began but was cut off by the door to the bedroom being thrown open by Edward and Thomas Egerton.

"Now come, this is not the task you were assigned,"

Thomas sighed as he marched over to his cousin and unceremoniously parted the pair.

"My lady, our deepest apologies for our cousin's lack of manners and self-preservation. We will do our best to educate him on the former, but the latter may already be a lost cause. I would like to take the opportunity to offer you our most sincerest assurances this won't happen again," Edward bowed to Lady Sarah, revealing Sylvia stood in the corridor behind them looking thoroughly unimpressed.

Thomas and Edward removed Oliver from the room as Lady Sarah did her best to stifle the laughter she felt welling up inside her.

Sylvia scowled at Oliver as he was dragged past her and marched into the room, closing the door behind her.

"You are a truly terrifying woman. You have both Thomas and Edward afraid of you already," Lady Sarah giggled as she sat down beside Bronwyn.

"Then I still have much work to do," Sylvia replied with a shrug.

"What did the doctor say?" Sarah asked as she took Bronwyn's hand in hers and gently stroked it.

"He said that we need to clean and redress her

wounds, make sure the bedpan gets emptied, and if it spills, we have to call for one of the men to lift her up whilst we change the sheets. She needs to be washed and any time she awakens, he will come and give her something for her pain.," Sylvia replied as she looked around the room to see where everything lived.

The bedpan, she discovered, was nothing more than a tray pushed into the bed underneath Bronwyn.

"I think perhaps we need to send for some better bedpans and more sheets," Sylvia sighed.

"I am sure Miss DeVille can send some of the farmhands to fetch them. If you tell her what you need, or perhaps she can even go herself," Lady Sarah suggested.

Sylvia nodded and left Lady Sarah with Bronwyn whilst she went to find Miss DeVille.

Derwyn had taken his fiancée to the kitchen to show her all that his mother did during the day from cooking meals to cleaning, then out into the farmyard to show her everything that Bronwyn did there, from feeding the ducks and chickens, collecting the eggs, milking the cows for the milk for the house to the dirty jobs she would tackle.

Miss DeVille was thrilled when Sylvia approached

her to ask her to go in search of supplies for the house. Before they had left Grangeback, the brigadier had entrusted Sylvia with a sum of money that was to be used to pay for whatever expenses had to be covered. Lady Sarah had paid for the rooms at the inn from her own purses, and the Egertons had paid for the meals they had eaten, so Sylvia had yet to dip into the brigadier's funds. She brought out a few guineas and pounds and gave them to Miss DeVille to buy as much as she could from the list that Sylvia gave her.

Though Derwyn agreed that they needed the items, he did not like having to end his tour of his mother's responsibilities to take Miss DeVille to the nearest village, but there was little else to be done.

The pair set off in the farm trap pulled by one of the stocky ponies that was used to help plough some of the more uneven fields.

Sylvia stood in the farmyard and sighed to herself. There was much to be done to simply keep the farm from falling apart whilst Bronwyn was in bed, let alone for the group to search properly for the missing girls.

She wondered what would happen if they failed in

their task and if Gordon would be able to accept that the two women were gone forever. She wondered how Lady Sarah would react. It would grow dark soon enough and the search party would be forced to return. Sylvia hoped for their success, though she was not certain there could be any.

But her hopes were soon pushed to the back of her mind as she had other concerns at present, namely the care of the woman upon whom the foundation of the farm seemed to be built.

Chapter 14

Mr Alexander Hunter rode at the back of the group. He did not know the country well enough to ride from the front. The bandits turned farmhands rode beside Gordon, the doctor's son knew the countryside well and could navigate the place in the dark.

The other farmhands rode in the middle, ready to chase after the bandits if they ran or make a correction to their course if they felt that they were being led astray.

They rode at a trot, brisk but easily manageable for the horses to maintain for a good distance. On the roads, they slowed to a walk so they wouldn't churn up the muck too much.

Mr Hunter had considered suggesting the group journey back to Hawarden and Ashdown, but there seemed little point in the group going over the ground already covered. Instead, they struck further into Wales. There were clusters of trees to traverse, but for the most part, the countryside was open and easy enough for the horses to traverse.

There were great hills that led down into great valleys, a dramatic and beautiful, but lost on the group who were searching for more than just scenery that belonged on a canvas.

As they descended down into the next valley over from the farm, they found themselves in a copse of trees that made it difficult for them to ride side-by-side.

Forced to single file, the trees soon made it difficult for one man to see the back of another through the branches. The trees and undergrowth became so dense that it became impossible for them to continue in the direction that they were headed.

Directions were shouted from one man to the next in a loud chain of Chinese whispers, but with each passing of the directions, a small detail was changed until there were three groups of riders spread out in the trees. Gordon, one of the bandits and one of the farmhands found themselves alone on the far side of the forest and chose to press on in their search.

The other bandit and farmhand found themselves to

the west of the trees and soon saw their compatriots riding away, so made to join up with them again.

But Mr Hunter was not so fortunate. He found himself in a small clearing, alone and with no clue of which direction to go in or where they had come from.

He knew that even if he was separated from the men, for now, they would likely double back for him, but in order to be found, he needed to locate the road they had come in on.

He patted Black Guy's neck and rubbed his forehead as he tried to work out the best direction for him to travel.

He couldn't see the sun through the trees, but the small shadows that were cast into the clearing told him which direction he was facing. He had travelled south in the forest and knew he needed to go back towards the east to reach the farm.

He turned Black Guy 90 degrees and urged him forward. It was dark to his left as he rode and made him think that he was on the right track back. He kept riding with the dense forest to his left until he found the trees too thick for Black Guy to pass any further.

There was no possibility he could break through the

trees to his left, so he wheeled the horse away to his right and pushed on, looking for a way through.

He seemed to have been riding for hours when there was a break in the trees and Black Guy was finally able to make it through in the direction Mr Hunter wanted to ride, but rather than finding himself in familiar surroundings, he found himself in front of a grand old house with a ramshackle wall around it.

It has a small garden that was overgrown in places, but in others, it looked well-cared for. The house itself was in need of some loving care and repairs and looked like a house that came from the tales about witches that his mother had told to him when he was a boy only, it had three storeys and no tower.

He looked up at the house from the saddle of Lady Sarah's horse, and for a moment could swear that he saw the familiar form of Millie in the uppermost window.

She was there only for a second and in the light bouncing off the window there was some room for doubt in his mind, but he was almost certain that it was her.

A rush of elation surged through his body at the thought that he found at least Millie, if not Grace as well. He held the great cheer he wanted to let out in his chest as the realisation sunk in that he had no idea where he was or how he would get back to the farm.

The only guidepost he had was the sun and he needed to think of a way to mark the way back so that if he did manage to find the farm or the others, he would be able to lead them back again.

He took out the small knife he carried for hunting and made his way around the edge of the trees to where he thought he needed to go. He marked one tree with a circle with a cross through it so that he would know where to go and was about to nudge Black Guy onwards when he felt gruff hands seize him and drag him from the horse.

Two men dragged him to the ground, and the bigger and rougher looking of the two men subdued Alex on the ground, the lither man went to grab the reins of Black Guy.

The Friesian stallion was not about to be handled by a man that had assaulted his rider. He reared, flashed giant hooves at the man who dared to get too close, and as the man recoiled, Black Guy spun and took off through the trees, as fast as the undergrowth would allow.

Mr Hunter watched the horse go as the trees tore at

the leather of the reins, and stirrups. They would be ruined long before the horse made it home.

The rough man brought a fist towards Alex's face and then there was nothing but darkness. When he opened his eyes again, he was no longer outside, but tied to a low wooden bed with an uncomfortable straw mattress. His head felt like it had been split open and his mouth was dry.

He tried to sit up but found that the bonds around his hands and feet wouldn't allow for it.

He sighed to himself and looked around as best he could. There was a single candle on the small wooden table beside the bed and a bowl of water with a washcloth lying in it.

Beyond the light of the candle, Alex could barely make out a dark figure that was busy doing something in the corner of the room.

He lay back without a sound and waited for the figure to do whatever it was they were there for.

"Mr Hunter, it has been quite some time," the figure said, and to Alex's relief, Grace stepped into the light and sat on the bed beside him.

She looked much thinner than she had the last time

he had seen her. She looked tired and there was a light missing from her eyes that had once shone so brightly there.

"Grace, you're alive!" Mr Hunter gasped with relief and tried to smile at her, but instead ended up wincing in pain.

"Try not to move too much, they did a lot of damage with their fists, well I expect that Mr Beets was the one who did all this to you. Mr Land is dangerous but he's not quick to use violence if he doesn't have to," Grace soothed as she reached for the bowl with the washcloth and used the cloth to drip some water into the hunter's mouth.

He was grateful for the liquid in his dry mouth but it tasted stale and warm.

"You know their names?" Alex asked with surprise after he had gulped down the water.

"Yes, I don't expect they thought we would ever leave their care alive so why not tell us their names? Not that we are anything other than servants here. But it has not been that bad. They have not hurt me too badly, and Mr Land has made sure Mr Beets didn't steal what little virtue I have remaining, " Grace shrugged.

Mr Hunter frowned and looked at the fear and

shadows on Grace's face and knew that she was lying. She had clearly endured much punishment at the hands of the two men and some of that torture would certainly haunt her for the rest of her life. It was clear that no matter what, Alex needed to take her away from the house, and soon.

"What about Millie? How is she?" Mr Hunter asked.

"I don't know,' Grace sighed, "I have not seen her since we were taken. I don't even know if she is in this house. I am allowed to go in certain rooms and that is all. I do what I am told and I sleep. I don't even know how long it has been since we were taken," Grace said sadly, for a moment Mr Hunter could see the pain and sadness of the whole situation etched in every contour of her body, but Grace closed her eyes and gathered it all back behind the shield she had been surviving behind.

"It has been almost a year. We have not stopped looking for you from the moment you were taken, her ladyship wouldn't allow us to stop. The police have been searching, our friends have been searching, I am here now because we had word you were close by, and lo, here you are," Mr Hunter said softly. Grace creased her brow as she felt tears threatening to burst forth, and did all she could to control them.

"And Millie is alive. I saw her at the top window when I found the house," Alex said gently. Grace could not hold back the flow of tears and fell on the groundskeeper's chest, weeping silently. Alex wished he could comfort her, but he knew that it was best to let her cry and let out all the emotion she had been denying for so long.

He did not know how long she cried, but when she stopped, she looked a great deal more drained than she had done before.

"Tell me everything that has happened since I last saw you, I have tried not to think of you all," Grace smiled weakly. She moved from the edge of the bed to sit on the floor and lean her back against the bed frame. She did not want Mr Hunter to see her face as she listened.

She wanted to keep her emotions to herself, after all, they were the last freedom she had open to her.

Mr Hunter spoke of everything that had happened, including the things that he knew would shock and scandalise the young woman. She listened to the tale of his love for Lady Sarah, of the lost baby, of the murders, the witch, the departure of the brigadier, the Baker boys at

Grangeback, the tour of the north, Sylvia's arrival, the missing women from the hospital, Arwyn's brother and father arriving, his abandonment of Lady Sarah and finally the arrival of Mr Brown.

When he had finished he let Grace process everything she had heard and waited for some form of response from the woman.

"You treated my lady very badly" Grace chided him slowly, "But I am sure that she will forgive you. It may take her some time to trust you with her heart again, but I know she loves you very deeply."

"I am glad you think so," Mr Hunter smiled to himself.

"I have to go and make the dinner now. I will come back later. I have not told them who you are. For now, you are safe," Grace said as she rose from the floor and put the bowl of water back on the table.

Before Alex could say anything to her, she had crossed the room and shot through the door, closing it firmly behind her.

He lay staring at the ceiling wondering how he would escape the bonds that held him and just when his head would stop throbbing.

Chapter 15

Thae J. Land did not like how close they had come to discovery and knew that with the horse loose, others would come looking for its missing rider. He had only one course of action open to him.

He waited until the darkness had fallen and rode out to the Evans farm. It was not far from the house in the woods, but he did not want to be seen.

He waited around the back of the common lodging-house until he was sure no one was there and slipped through a partially open window. He sat on one of the beds and waited until a man opened the door.

He did not seem surprised to see Mr Land waiting for him.

"We may have another problem to take care of," Thae said without a tinge of emotion in his voice.

The man on the bed sighed and shook his head.

"What kind of problem? I have done everything

you've asked so far. I beat up that woman to stop the boss from telling everyone what he knows. I kept the farmhands busy all day with emergencies after that group left without warning this morning. What else is there that I am supposed to do?"

"The kind of problem that needs taking permanent care of. A problem caused by you not stopping those riders from leaving this morning. More direct action is now required," Thae said impatiently, through gritted teeth.

"I don't want to be part of this anymore. It was one thing when you just wanted information, but the attack on Bronwyn, and now this, I can't be part of it anymore," the man said as boldly as he could.

"If that is the case, then we have nothing more to talk about," Mr Land said decisively as he stood and walked towards the window, "Of course, the police will be here shortly to arrest you. So I would ensure all your affairs are in order."

"What do you mean?" the man asked nervously.

"If you no longer wish to aid us, then you are of no more use to us. We have no need or reason to protect you and so we shall remove you and find someone else willing to help us," Thae shrugged.

"Wait, what do you need me to do?" the man asked with defeat and hung his head as Mr Land turned from the window and made his way back to the bed.

"We had an unexpected visitor at the house. A man that we say in Hawarden and Ashdown, a man that came from this farm. We have taken him prisoner, but it has made it abundantly clear that the attack on the lady of the farm was not enough to prevent the inconvenient investigations. We now need a more permanent solution," Thae said with a wry smile curling at the corner of his mouth.

"What kind of solution?" the man sighed.

"That solution is up to you. Whatever way you think best to kill them," Mr Land said simply.

"Kill them!" the man stuttered, his eyes wide with disbelief.

"Of course, my dear Simon, what did you think I meant by permanent solution?" Thae laughed at the naivety of his pawn.

The farmhand, known as Simon, could not find any words in the face of the task before him.

"There are several ways you can make it seem like an

accident. Poisoning is best, nice and easy for it to seem like someone was a bit careless with a chemical and it was introduced into the milk. You can do the job by hand, but make sure you leave any weapon in the hand of one of the occupants. I would suggest you use this," he said as he reach into his coat and pulled out a small vial, "It's an effective little poison, acts quickly and makes it look like a natural death. That way it doesn't look suspicious, more like a sudden outbreak of disease that wipes out a whole farm. A manhunt for a murderer would only draw more attention to us," Mr Land smiled and stood again.

"When do I need to do this?" Simon asked with a trembling voice.

"As soon as possible. Mr Beets will visit in three days' time. If they are not dead by then, you will be, and I will find another man who can accomplish the task," Thae said shortly and slipped out of the window without a sound.

He stopped in the cold night air and listened to the sound of Simon letting out a defeated sigh. Satisfied that there was nothing else to be done, he slipped away through the night, making sure he stayed downwind of the farm.

He knew that there was the dog to worry about, but as long as he kept to the shadows and downwind of the house, he would not be detected.

Mr Land felt no shred of pity for Simon. The man was foolish and stupid and had been willing to do anything for greed. In fact, far from feeling pity for the man, he felt a strange sense of satisfaction that even if he managed to kill the occupants of the house, Mr Beets would kill him anyway. There was no room for any form of loose ends in their enterprise.

He arrived back at the house in the woods without incident and made his way to the kitchen. He could smell food being prepared and was glad that he had not missed dinner. Grace was stood by the stove, working diligently to prepare their meal.

Mr Beets was sat by the fire, staring into the flames and absently playing with a dagger in his hands.

"Well?" Mr Beets asked without shifting his gaze from the fireplace.

"It has been taken care of. Simon has three days to kill them before you pay him a visit. Be sure to take him away from the farm and kill him somewhere near the border. We don't want to make it look too suspicious," Mr Land said dryly as he took off his overcoat and made his way to the dinner table.

He briefly paused behind Grace long enough to grab her hips and smell her hair. It was something of a ritual that had become part of Grace's daily life. She was not just there to satisfy their need for food and drink, but whatever other needs that Mr Land wanted.

Mr Beets had never shown any interest in her in such a way, perhaps because of Mr Land's claim to her body, but he often visited taverns and would stay out all night instead.

When Mr Land had first forced his intentions on Grace she had quivered and flinched at the very sight of him. Now she had accepted it as what it was, another fact of her existence. There was no love or desire on her part, nor any love on his part, simply the desire for power of another human being forced to do whatever he wanted.

"What about the man upstairs, what are we going to do about him?" Mr Beets asked impatiently.

"We shall dispose of him when we are sure that we know everything he does. You can begin interrogating him

in the morning, just make sure you don't kill him too soon,"
Mr Land said with a wave of his hand.

Grace served the dinner giving no indication that
she had heard anything or felt anything about the plans of
the two men. She waited until they had finished eating, and
then cleared away their dishes.

She took Mr Hunter some broth and fed him without
saying a word.

When Mr Land came to her room in the dead of
night and took what he wanted from her, she did not resist
or squirm, she did not recoil or question. After he was
finished with her and left her for the warmth of his own
bed, she did not sleep. Instead, she sat on the edge of her
bed and listened intently to the sounds of the house.

Eventually, she was sure that all she could hear was
the rhythmic breathing of those asleep. Without wasting a
moment she slipped out of her room and went down to the
kitchen to fetch a knife.

She moved quickly and silently, making her way to
the room where Mr Hunter was being held. She used the tip
of the knife to help ease the knots so that she could untie
them without ripping her fingernails.

Any sign that she had helped Mr Hunter escape would lead to severe punishment, but she would not let him be tortured and killed.

"Grace, what are you doing?" Mr Hunter asked drowsily as he felt the lessening of the strain on his arms and legs.

"Quick, you must be quick and quiet. Go back to the farm, they are all in great danger. Please, do not let them kill them," Grace whispered urgently.

"What are you talking about?" Mr Hunter tried to soothe her.

"There is no time, please, go now and save them. You must save them all," Grace begged.

"You must come with me, I cannot leave you here with these men," Mr Hunter replied as he sat up and fought the desire to call out in pain as the blood flow returned to his arms and legs and the muscles were finally able to move.

"I cannot, not without Millie. There isn't time to rescue us now, you have to get back to the farm before morning. We will be fine here until you come back for us. Now please, go," Grace urged and helped the groundskeeper to his feet.

It took a moment for Mr Hunter to find he could walk without collapsing, even if he could only move slowly. Grace helped him through the house, her ears pricked for the slightest sound that would tell her someone in the house was stirring.

Once out in the cold night air, Grace waved goodbye and hurried back to her bed. The knife lying forgotten in Mr Hunter's room.

Mr Hunter felt much better to be free of the house, and glad there were no dogs to warn of his escape. He rushed through the trees surrounding the edge of the glade the house lay in. He marked the path as best he could, digging his fingers in to tear away at the bark of certain trees as he passed.

It was almost dawn when he finally reached the edge of the trees and found a familiar path and rushed down it, hoping that he was not too late.

Chapter 16

The night had fallen by the time that Gordon and the riders from the farm arrived back at the farm. Black Guy had arrived many hours before and been stabled.

Gordon had assumed, when Hunter did not join them, that he had turned back and ridden home rather than risk getting lost in the wilds of Wales.

When he found Black Guy in the stables, in his mind, his suspicions were confirmed. It wasn't until he walked despondently up to the farmhouse that he realised that anything was wrong.

"Is he with you?" Lady Sarah asked with worry the moment that Gordon opened the door.

"Who? Hunter? Of course not, we lost him when we got separated in the trees. He's not here?" Gordon replied with a frown creasing his forehead.

"No, Black Guy came back without him a number of hours ago. We hoped that the horse had been spooked and bolted for home leaving Hunter riderless, but still with you," Richard told his brother.

Lady Sarah's face was rather drawn with worry and her skin had lost all its usual colour. Mr Brown sat beside her, holding her hand, but she didn't even seem to notice the man was there.

"Then we must set out to find him," Edward said decisively.

"Not tonight," the doctor said firmly and all eyes turned to him. Jack Hales could see the confusion in the eyes of his companions, and though he wanted to find Mr Hunter as much as any of them did, he knew that the risk of searching for him was far too great.

"It is dark and most of you do not know the country. Hunter is a survivor. If he fell and is injured, he will have made a shelter or devised some form of way of getting back here, albeit slowly. If something more nefarious has happened or worse, then charging about in the dark will do little to help him and put everyone in more danger than they are already in," he said gently and watched as understanding crept over each face before him.

"You are right, of course, doctor," Thomas shrugged

and sighed.

"We cannot just leave him out there," Lady Sarah protested.

"And we won't. But we must wait until the morning when we can look for tracks and trails and enlist the help of others to search for him. No, come, my lady, I think you need to rest," the doctor soothed and took her hand from Mr Brown.

He helped her to her feet and led her toward the stairs.

The farmhouse was big and old, but it was not suited to providing all of its current guests with private rooms. Lady Sarah, Miss DeVille and Sylvia all shared the smaller back room that doubled as Bronwyn's sewing room.

Spare beds had been carried over from the common lodging-house so that no one had to sleep on the floor.

Bronwyn was to have the master bedroom to herself whilst she healed, though Edryd refused to sleep anywhere except in the chair by her bed.

The other three bedrooms were divided between the men, and the Baker Boys opted to sleep downstairs with Pattinson to act as guards with the dog, should anyone try to break into the house in the dead of night, the pair and hound would make enough noise to raise the dead.

"Let me take her, doctor," Sylvia smiled as she took his place at her side and helped her mistress to climb the stairs.

"Thank you, Sylvia," the doctor said with sincerity and waited until he heard the door to the room upstairs open and close before he spoke again.

"When the horse came back early, Derwyn, you were ready to set out and search for Hunter, what stopped you?" the doctor asked as he began to slowly pace around the kitchen.

"As you know, it was not long past lunch when we saw Lady Sarah's horse come trotting back here without him, and there were plenty of us on hand to go and search. We had the horses ready and were about to set out when there was a problem in the lambing fields and a small fire started in the hay barn. If we hadn't all been here, we wouldn't have gotten things under control so quickly, but by the time we had cleared everything away, it was getting dark and we decided to wait for Gordon and the others to come back before we went rushing around in the dark,"

Derwyn explained.

"And who was it that told you about the lambing problem and discovered the fire?" the doctor asked suspiciously, "Was it the same man?"

"Yes, it was Simon Farrow. He's been here for years though. He's a solid enough worker. Likes a bit of a drink and the odd flutter, but no real vice in him," Derwyn said dismissively.

"He likes to gamble?" Arwyn asked as he stood up from his seat by the fire, looking concerned.

"Who among the farmhands doesn't like to put a bob or two on a race now and then?" Derwyn laughed at his brother's interest in the farmhand's hobby.

"How much has he lost?" Arwyn asked patiently.

"God only knows, it's been so long since he came back with winnings to splash around, I can hardly remember," Derwyn shrugged.

"I see," the doctor said grimly.

"Come now, you can't suspect a man because he lost a few quid on the nags," Derwyn said with a shake of his head.

"I think we have every right to suspect this man of a

great many things. But for now, we have nothing more than suspicions. Perhaps you could point out this man to Stanley and Lee in the morning and have the pair follow him for the day," the doctor suggested.

"If you say so, doctor, but it will all come to nought," Derwyn said jovially.

"Perhaps it will, but will Mr Hunter missing, I would rather be safe than sorry and keep anyone that is even marginally suspicious under a close and watchful eye," Jack sighed.

"Come now, enough of this talk, it is time for dinner. Arwyn, would you be kind enough to take some up for Sylvia and her ladyship?" Miss DeVille said breaking across the conversation and trying her utmost to look as though she were enjoying the menial kitchen tasks she had been assigned.

"Of course," Arwyn agreed and did as he was bid.

Dinner was a more subdued affair with Mr Hunter absent. Most had their minds occupied by thoughts of betrayal and who was to blame, but Mr Brown's head was full of dark thoughts of guilt and remorse.

He had wanted Mr Hunter out of the way, to be free

of the groundskeeper so that the American could spend more time with her ladyship without his influence.

Now his wish to see Mr Hunter disappear had been granted, and as irrational as his guilt was, he couldn't help but feel that Alex's disappearance was all his fault.

Chapter 17

The peaceful sleep that should have reigned at the farm that night was broken by great howls of pain coming from the common lodging-house.

If the cries of pain hadn't carried so far to wake the house, the relentless banging on the door of frightened fists would have been more than enough.

The doctor, Derwyn and Arwyn rushed over to the common lodging-house accompanied by one of the men that had ridden out with Gordon that day.

Everyone else was to wait in the farmhouse with the doors bolted to protect the ladies, just in case the emergency was some form of distraction.

The three men rushed out into the night with the rider, the doctor with his bag in hand. By the time that they reached the common lodging-house, three men had collapsed and were crying in pain. They were suffering from great fevers that had come on suddenly.

Every man that the doctor spoke to had not noticed anything strange or different about their comrades whilst they had eaten dinner, but once the meal had finished, the three men in question had all felt tired and retreated to their beds.

None of the other men were showing any of the same symptoms as the sick men, but they had all eaten the same food and drunk from the same jug. There was nothing that explained why these three men were so suddenly and violently ill.

Arwyn and Derwyn oversaw the movement of the three men into a room together, just in case the illness was infectious.

"What can be done?" the constable asked in a low voice when the door to the room containing the three men was closed.

"I will try to purge the fever, but I will need to release blood from them to do it. I would rather not do it close to the pregnant animals, so we may have to have the men moved. If they were able to sit up and talk, I would say we try to purge their stomachs first, but I am concerned they will choke. There is not much I can do for them tonight. We can only pray that they last the night and do what we can do them in the morning," Jack sighed and rubbed his head.

"Do you have any idea what caused such a sudden fever?" Derwyn asked in equally hushed tones.

"None. If we were in a hotter climate, I would consider it to be malaria or some such malady, but here, it is impossible to say," the doctor sighed.

"I think her ladyship might disagree," Arwyn said grimly and shook his head.

"And I believe we would be best not to speak of the fever to her. Her parents and everyone in her household were taken by a fever," the doctor warned.

"All the more reason she should be informed. She was the only one to survive the fever and to have this happen again, it seems too much to be a coincidence," Arwyn replied thoughtfully.

"Perhaps, but I would be concerned about the impact on her sanity after all that has happened, and with Mr Hunter missing, I am not sure that it would not be all too much for her," the doctor said thoughtfully.

"There is no reason to lie to her now, she will find out one way or another. Telling her now would be the best idea," Derwyn replied.

The doctor sighed deeply and then nodded in agreement.

One man was left to sit outside of the door and make sure that no one went in or out of the room until the doctor came back in the morning.

The three men made their way back to the farmhouse in silence, each considering the events of the day and what it all meant.

Lady Sarah was waiting for the three men in the kitchen when they returned. The rest of the house was up and anxious for news as well.

"So doctor, what has happened?" Lady Sarah asked with a steady voice.

"A sudden fever in three of the men. The two bandits that had joined us after we found them in that cave, and one of the riders that accompanied us," the doctor said firmly and watched Lady Sarah closely for her reaction.

"I see, then it is Lady de Mandeville who is behind all this," she sighed with a clenched fist in her lap.

"Lady de Mandeville?" Mr Brown frowned in confusion.

"Our nemesis, and the particular enemy of Lady Sarah. She is a powerful woman with many powerful friends, and is not above destroying the lives of those that stand in her way," Edward replied with a grim expression.

"She is not above taking lives either," Thomas added.

"She is the woman who had my parents killed. They and all those in our household in India contracted a mysterious fever that killed them all. I was the only one to survive. The countess discovered that the fever was caused by a virulent poison that was created in the subcontinent. For it to have surfaced here leads to the only conclusion, Lady de Mandeville is behind these poisonings, the kidnapping of Grace and Millie, and the disappearance of Mr Hunter," Lady Sarah's voice wavered as she spoke.

"Then we should find out the source of the poison in the morning, until then, we should try to get some rest," the doctor said and began ushering everyone out of the room.

Chapter 18

The sun was casting weak light as it rose the following morning. Mr Hunter struggled into the farmyard and had never been more glad to see any place in his life.

His body ached, and his head swam, but he had survived his capture and escape and managed to find his way back through unfamiliar territory.

He was greeted by the sound of barking as he approached the house and the eager Pattinson bounded over to greet his master.

Some of the farmhands were already at work milking the cows in the large shed that lay on one side of the yard, and not long after Pattinson had greeted him, the Baker Boys, Arwyn and Derwyn were beside him, helping the groundskeeper to keep his feet as they made their way around to the kitchen door.

Miss DeVille was struggling to prepare breakfast for the house, but Sylvia was with her, offering a limited instruction on how to cook, something that was only causing more frustration for Miss DeVille.

Both women were surprised when the kitchen door was flung open by Stanley Baker as he raced in to pull out one of the chairs from the table for Mr Hunter to collapse in.

Derwyn began shouting for things and stared at the two women when neither of them moved. Instead, Lee Baker began to run frantically around looking for everything that Derwyn was calling for.

Lady Sarah and the doctor were both with Bronwyn in the main room, but the sound of the commotion in the kitchen drew them quickly downstairs.

Thomas, Edward and Mr Brown sleepily opened their door to see Lady Sarah and the doctor fly past their door. Richard and Gordon were both in the study talking about the possibility of a traitor amongst the farmhands but abandoned their train of thought to investigate the commotion.

"What the devil is happening down there?" Edward yawned.

"Mr Hunter has returned," Stanley shouted back as he ran up the stairs in search of a good blanket to wrap around the groundskeeper's shoulders.

"I say!" Thomas exclaimed and ran ahead of his brother and cousin to be the first of the three in the kitchen.

Lady Sarah was sat in a chair opposite to Mr Hunter, her back straight, her hands folded neatly in her lap, but with a distinct look of relief on her face.

The doctor was examining the young man and taking great care to not overlook any aspect of his anatomy.

Miss DeVille had returned to her attempt of creating breakfast whilst most eyes were distracted by the sudden appearance of Mr Hunter.

"Where have you been, Hunter?" Richard asked with affection as he stood by Lady Sarah's shoulder, beaming at his friend.

"In a dark dark house, in a dark, dark wood," Mr Hunter managed to reply as he steadied his breathing.

"What on earth happened to you in those trees?" Gordon asked with a frown.

"When I lost the rest of you, I tried to double back but had to go a long way wrong. I ended up in a clearing in the forest where a run-down, ramshackle old house sits. It wouldn't be worth mentioning but Grace and Millie are both there. I saw them. Well Millie I saw through a window. Grace took care of me when her kidnappers captured me. She helped me to escape so that I could warn you, that the men are trying to have you killed. She wouldn't leave without Millie, but I fear for her safety, as they are certain to know she freed me," Mr Hunter replied.

"We must go at once!" Gordon blurted out, but Thomas and Edward grabbed each of his shoulders and held the man steady.

"We will go, but first, we must discover how exactly these men planned to kill us," Thomas said flatly.

"The poison, the fever, someone here is a traitor and I fear that the poison last night was merely the start of what is to come. We must find the man behind it at once," Richard said decisively.

"Mr Hunter will be taking to a bed for a few hours, so your investigations must be conducted without him, Lady Sarah, I think it best that you and Sylvia should stay here and take care of Mr Hunter and Bronwyn," the doctor said firmly, offering neither Mr Hunter nor Lady Sarah any recourse or forum for protest.

"Gordon and I will guard the house with Pattinson, I

am sure my father will need to go visit the three men from last night, the rest of you should go and question the farmhands. Miss DeVille, I am sure will reward us with a fine breakfast once we are finished," Richard smiled at the woman and received a grateful grin in response.

"An excellent plan, but to question the farmhands, we must all dress," Mr Brown said with a wry smile as he looked at his cousins, who were both still in their nightshirts.

"True, true, we shall be ready by the time Hunter has been put to bed," Thomas grinned.

Edward nodded at the groundskeeper with a warm smile, relief at his friend's return was etched into every contour of his expression.

"Gordon, Richard, if you would be so good as to take our injured friend to his room and ensure that he stays in his bed, I will take Lady Sarah and Sylvia to visit with our sick charges before the interrogation can begin," Jack Hales said, not shifting his eyes from Mr Hunter.

"No, I must come and help you," Mr Hunter protested as he tried to fight off the hands of Richard and Gordon that tried to help him to his feet.

"Alex, you will do as the doctor orders. I will not have you leave this house until you have slept," Lady Sarah said sharply. The authority in her voice was not lacking warmth or affection, but it was so rare for her to raise her voice, or to speak sternly that she shocked the groundskeeper into a brief submission.

Richard and Gordon seized upon the moment to grab hold of Hunter and haul with to his feet, an arm around each of their necks, walking him hurriedly up the stairs to his room.

Thomas, Edward and Oliver follow behind the trio in a rush to dress and return to join the manhunt for the traitor.

Lady Sarah waited until she heard the door to Mr Hunter's room open before she rose to her feet and instructed Pattinson to guard the house.

"Good boy," she said as she patted the great animal's head as he sat with his ears pricked and his eyes firmly trained on the door to the kitchen.

"We'll come with you!" Stanley and Lee chorused as they rushed forward and took Lady Sarah by the hand, one boy on either side.

"You are so very kind to me," she smiled at the two boys, who blushed with delight.

"Then it seems you shall be my escort, doctor," Sylvia said with a spark of humour in her eyes.

"A duty I will accept with great joy," the doctor replied with the same entertained look on his face.

It was odd to all of them to think that the two boys would no longer be living at the manor, they had brought such life and mischief to the great house in the absence of their mother, but it was only right that they return to her home and begin their apprenticeships in whatever field they would make their future careers. This was their last time being merely boys who were unburdened enough to play games in the streets and go off on wild adventures.

Neither of the two boys seemed to have registered or even considered that this would be their last opportunity to live so freely, they were simply swept up in the moment, enjoying the mystery, wherever it lead them.

The five left Miss DeVille to prepare the breakfast in peace without the pressure of anyone looking over her shoulder or offering her any unwanted advice.

She knew she could manage much better without

Sylvia at her side, especially since there would be almost no interference from Richard or Gordon when it came to cooking.

The walk down to the common lodging-house was a pleasant one. Lady Sarah seemed to have had a great weight lifted from her shoulders with Mr Hunter's return, and even the prospect of seeing men afflicted as her parents and those of her childhood home were with the effects of such a virulent poison, did nothing to dampen her mood.

There was a slight chill in the air, but the sun was warm and bright, casting weak rays onto the frost that clung to the corners of the farmhouse and the cobbles on the ground. The frost sparkled and danced creating beautiful patterns that one could get lost in if there were not so many other things to occupy the mind.

The dance of the frost was not lost on the Baker boys, but to Sylvia, it was a welcome relief that this was another day when she had not woken to such a frost clinging to her clothing.

She had been lucky enough not to have spent many nights sleeping on the streets of Chester, begging for food and clinging to whatever warmth could be found, but they had been the bitter nights of an early winter that had already claimed the lives of many who lived their lives sheltering in doorways or in homes that could not keep out the biting cold.

The frost was a grim reminder of where she had been and could easily be again should her patrons decide that she was not welcome any longer.

Lady Sarah and Doctor Hales were both deep in thought as they crossed the cobbles and neither paid much attention to their surroundings, other than to be careful where they placed their feet.

It would be a few weeks yet before the cold from the air became the warm summer winds, but the rains would come soon. The spring rains would wash away the last vestiges of winter and cause the riot of colour that would spring forth from the ground in the shape of snowdrops, daffodils, bluebells, roses and many other flowers that would provide such a stark contrast to the dismal greys of winter.

The common lodging-house was much warmer than it had been the night before, and the doctor was relieved to discover that the three men were the only ones who had become sick.

None of the farmhands had eaten or drunk a thing that morning, out of fear of where the sickness had come from. The doctor had been careful to keep the news that it was poison far from the ears of the farmhands.

He did not wish to cause a panic or for the men to turn upon one another in an effort to find the poisoner.

Lady Sarah, Sylvia and the Baker boys gathered those not already at work in the dining area of the common lodging-house to talk to them all about what they could remember from the previous night.

The doctor went to see the three men whilst the questioning began and found that one of the three men had passed away in the night and that the other two were not far behind him.

He felt so helpless as he sat and looked at the two men. He could do nothing to ease their passing and understood a little better why Lady Sarah held so much pain in her heart over the deaths of her parents.

He waited with the two men, talking calmly to them, holding their hands to ease their passing. He did not stir from their bedsides until they had both gone beyond the veil and then covered each of the men in turn.

He would have their bodies collected later and if they had no family to pay for a burial he knew that Lady Sarah would insist on paying for a proper one for each man.

When he opened the door to the room, he found Arwyn waiting outside of it.

"Are they?" the constable asked in a low voice.

"Yes, all three. Whoever did this has gone from merely a saboteur to a fully-fledged murderer," the doctor said grimly.

"Why those three men though?" Arwyn wondered aloud.

"Two of them were the former bandits, the other one of the riders that searched the woods, I think we can surmise that the three of them were targeted on purpose, but I also think they were just the beginning. A test of the poison," Jack replied with a slight shake of his head.

"Then there are two targets that would seem to be rational next steps," the policeman sighed.

"Yes, the other rider and your mother," the doctor agreed.

Arwyn did not miss a beat, he set off running. He

skidded into the dining area with a wild look in his eyes. He scanned over the faces of the men there, hoping to see something that looked akin to guilt, but read nothing.

The doctor arrived moments behind him.

"Your ladyship, you and the constable are needed at the house. He will explain, but there is no time to lose. I will deal with things here," he said boldly.

Lady Sarah frowned slightly but gathered her wits quickly and set off with Arwyn. They could not run out on the frozen ground, which was all for the better as Lady Sarah could not easily run in the dress she wore.

"What is happening?" she asked as they walked as quickly as the ground allowed.

"The three poisoned men are dead. Two of them were the bandits that joined us after your capture of them, the other was one of the riders. The doctor thinks that they were chosen on purpose and were a test of the poison. He also thinks that the other rider and my mother are the next targets," Arwyn explained.

"Your mother was a message to your father, after her assault, killing her first would break your father and punish not only him but you and your brother for daring to interfere. The other rider I would have expected to have already been poisoned," Lady Sarah said slowly.

"He was not at the meal last night as he was helping me with the horses when they returned. I brought him something from the house after dinner. I suspect he would have been targeted if it had not been for that," Arwyn replied.

"Then it is food or water that has been poisoned. I suspect that water is far more likely. It is easier to poison a glass or pitcher of water than it is to poison a meal," Lady Sarah surmised.

Pattinson barked with joy as he caught the scent of his mistress on the breeze.

Richard and Gordon came out of the house to see what it was that had caught the attention of the dog.

"What is it?" Richard asked as he saw the lady and policeman approaching.

"Has anyone been to the house in our absence?" Lady Sarah called out as they struggled to cover the last section of the farmyard.

"Only Simon. He brought the milk to the house," Gordon replied.

"The milk!" Arwyn cried and wheeled around to rush back to the common lodging-house.

"Has anyone drunk it?" Lady Sarah demanded.

"No, not yet. We were going to have it with breakfast," Richard laughed nervously at the young lady's intensity.

"Ah, well we were, but Edryd took up Bronwyn's breakfast tray a moment ago with some for her," Gordon corrected his brother.

Lady Sarah pushed both men aside, gathering as much of her skirt as she could and ran up the few steps into the house.

She ignore the surprised shout from Miss DeVille and charged up the steps, taking them two at a time. Pattinson beside her.

Her lungs burned as the contrast between the cold and warm air mixing so suddenly could not be avoided, but she ignored the pain and pressed on.

She did not try to be quiet or dainty in her movements, something her mother would have been horrified by, and she created so much noise that Mr Hunter heaved himself from his bed in time to see Lady Sarah throw open the door to the bedroom.

Edryd had the glass of milk in his hand, in two strides, Lady Sarah had closed the distance between the door and the old man and struck the glass from it.

"What the devil?" Edryd demanded crossly.

"Did either of you drink it?" Lady Sarah asked urgently.

"No, you threw it all over the floor before I could give it to her," Edryd said angrily.

Pattinson slowly approached the milk on the floor, sniffed at it suspiciously and growled.

"Good boy," Lady Sarah said as she placed her hand on his collar and pulled him back from the spillage.

"Explain yourself," Edryd shouted.

"The milk was poisoned. I suspect that the whole pail was dosed with it," Lady Sarah said flatly as she released her skirts and swept from the room.

Mr Hunter stood in the hallway looking at her as she approached.

"Do you know who is behind it? Who the traitor is?" he asked in a low voice as she passed.

"I do, and you need to go rest," she said with mild

annoyance. He opened his mouth as though he would protest, but the look in Lady Sarah's eyes warned him not to.

Richard and Gordon were both waiting at the bottom of the stairs for the lady and the hound. Pattinson came clattering down first and went over to the milk to sniff the pail.

He growled at the metal bucket as Lady Sarah descended.

"The poison is in the milk, did anyone drink it?" Lady Sarah asked calmly.

"Only I did," Miss DeVille replied with a quaver in her voice.

"I'll go fetch my father and Derwyn," Richard said without hesitation.

"Have Stan and Lee milk the cows for some fresh milk too," Lady Sarah said stoically as she looked at Miss DeVille with pity.

"What do I do?" Miss DeVille asked with terror.

"Drink some water and then go lie down. The doctor will be here very soon. It has not been too long since you drank the milk, it may be that we have time to stop it," Lady

Sarah said kindly, though she did not believe her own words.

"What can I do?" Gordon asked worriedly.

"Take some water up for Bronwyn, have Pattinson check it first, just in case, and I will think of how best to deal with the milk," Lady Sarah frowned at the pail and wondered what to do with it.

She did not want to pour it down the sewer system, and she did not want to poison any of the farmland, but it could not sit forever in the bucket in the kitchen.

It did not take long for Richard to return with Derwyn and the doctor and the two rushed upstairs.

With all the activity in the house, it was impossible for Mr Hunter to rest, so he joined Lady Sarah and Richard in the kitchen as they pondered the milk.

Gordon came down not long after Mr Hunter with Edryd in tow.

"I must apologise, your Ladyship, you saved my wife's life," Edryd said sheepishly.

"Such a pity that I was not in time to save Miss DeVille," Lady Sarah shook her head as she spoke.

"Gordon told me. Perhaps the doctor will be able to

stop the effects of the poison," Edryd said hopefully.

"It is always a possibility," Lady Sarah sighed, "May I ask if you have an old tank that is disused somewhere on the farm? I wish to dispose of the milk but with the poison in it, I would rather we put it in something that simply pour it away or poison the ground."

"There is an old tank on the far side of the barn. We used to store water in it, but we could put the milk in there," Edryd replied.

"Very good, if you can show me where I can dispose of it now. We should probably do the same with the milk at the common lodging-house too," Richard said and went to pick up the pail. The two men left the kitchen, leaving Lady Sarah with Mr Hunter and Gordon.

"So who is the traitor?" Mr Hunter asked the moment the door to the kitchen closed behind Edryd and Richard.

"Arwyn will be bringing him up shortly, I have no doubt. You will see him for yourself then. I hope that Stanley and Lee come back with the milk before he does," Lady Sarah replied and the three lapsed into silence as they waited.

Almost twenty minutes passed before Stanley Baker came up to the house carrying a fresh pail of milk.

"Lee's taken one down to the common lodging-house, he'll be along shortly. There was a lot of shouting coming from there," Stanley reported as he set the pail down in the corner of the room.

"I am not surprised. Thank you for being so good as to milk the cows, you have both grown into life on the farm well," Lady Sarah smiled as she rose to her feet, patted Stanley on the head and picked up a rough cup from one of the kitchen shelves. She dipped it into the milk, wiped the excess from the outside with a cloth and placed it in the middle of the table.

Outside in the farmyard, the sound of shouting could be heard and it ricocheted off the buildings, making the noise even worse.

"Gentlemen, if you would be so kind as to sit in the chairs by the fire and give me the table. I know you both wish to exact a measure of vengeance on this man, but I must first ask him some questions. Please, be patient," Lady Sarah said gently and both Gordon and Mr Hunter did as they were asked.

Stanley stood beside Lady Sarah and was joined by Lee who burst through the kitchen door ahead of the others.

Arwyn was not alone in his escort of the traitor. Thomas, Henry, Sylvia, Mr Brown and Edward were with him as well as almost every man that worked on the farm. The kitchen swarmed with people, almost too many to allow Arwyn to bring the traitor through and place him in the chair at the table that was opposite Lady Sarah.

"Simon, so kind of you to join us," Lady Sarah said amiably and turned to whisper in Stanley's ear.

The boy edged around the table and moved the cup of milk from the centre of the table to sit directly in front of the farm labourer.

"Please, drink some," Lady Sarah said with an edge of menace to her voice.

Simon looked at the milk and looked back at her.

"No, thank you," he replied as calmly as he could.

"Come now, I insist," Lady Sarah smiled dangerously at him.

"No, thank you," Simon said again, but with less composure.

"Arwyn, it seems our guest is struggling to accept

our gracious hospitality, perhaps you would be so good as to help him," Lady Sarah asked the constable in a sickly sweet voice.

Simon leapt out of the chair and was gripped by arms by the farmhands that were waiting for him.

Arwyn picked up the glass of milk from the table and walked grimly over to where Simon was being held.

"You can't!" Simon screamed, "It will kill me!"

"Why ever would a glass of milk kill you?" Lady Sarah feigned ignorance as Arwyn stopped in front of the struggling man.

"It's poisoned, I poisoned it to kill all of you," Simon cried.

"Yes, we are aware of that. But that milk is not from you poisoned pail," Lady Sarah said icily.

Arwyn threw the milk in Simon's face in disgust and motioned for the men to bring him back to the table. The two farmhands dragged him back and pushed him down into the chair and held him there.

"You have just admitted to attempted murder in front of all these witnesses. Did you kill the three men at the common lodging-house last night with poison?" Lady Sarah asked civilly.

"Yes," Simon said.

"Then it is murder too. On whose orders?" Lady Sarah demanded.

"A man came to the farm, he said his name was Land, he had a friend called Mr Beets with him. Mr Beets looked like a common street thug, but Mr Land had the airs of a gentleman. They offered me money, to help with my gambling debts. I was desperate. They only wanted small things at first, but when Mr Evans sent that letter to bring you all here, they found out somehow and were so cross I thought they were going to kill me. They said they wouldn't if I helped them stop Mr Evans from helping you. So," Simon explained.

"So you were the one who hurt Bronwyn," Lady Sarah finished for him.

"Yes," Simon swallowed hard and looked at the men around him with fear. The pressure the two men on either side of him had placed on his shoulders was increasing and had reached painful levels.

"Constable, I believe we are in need of a policeman's expertise in this matter. I doubt he is going to be able to leave the farm and get very far, but I would like things to be official," Lady Sarah said with an air of satisfaction.

"Take him out to the barn, we can lock him in the hayloft and put him under guard until we are ready to take him to Chester," Arwyn instructed the farmhands who all clamoured amongst themselves to be the ones to help drag the traitor out of the house.

"Will he live to see Chester?" Mr Brown asked with a frown.

"Perhaps, but if not, is he really such a great loss?" Gordon shrugged in reply.

"I will go tell my brother, and my father," Arwyn said with a shake of his head.

"Your father will see him on his way back from the barn. I expect he will be told by the men what happened. Stay with your brother for now," Lady Sarah said gently.

"What is it that you are going to do?" Arwyn frowned at the young lady.

"Go and rescue Grace and Millie so we can take them home. We've waited long enough," Lady Sarah said firmly.

"We'll get the horses ready," Lee and Stanley

volunteered and rushed out of the door. Lady Sarah smiled and rose from the table.

"Sylvia, I believe we will need to be dressed a little differently for this expedition," she smiled and the two women went upstairs to change.

"Constable, a moment, when you were threatening that man with the cup of milk, did you know that it wasn't poisoned?" Mr Brown asked with a worried look on his face.

"I did," Arwyn replied with a grunt.

"But how?" Mr Brown furrowed his brow.

"Lady Sarah lost her parents and all of her household to the same poison. She wouldn't wish that fate on her worst enemy, and that enemy is the one who used it on her family," Mr Hunter replied with a yawn.

"What if you hadn't known that it wasn't poisoned? Would you have done the same thing?" Mr Brown asked, earning a reproachful look from his cousins.

"We'll never know for sure," Arwyn shrugged.

"That is not an answer," Mr Brown insisted.

"It's the only one that you will get. If you'll excuse me I have my brother to look after," Arwyn said politely and excused himself from the conversation.

"Are you coming to rescue the ladies?" Mr Hunter asked as he watched Arwyn retreat up the stairs.

"Of course, why would I remain?" Mr Brown asked with hostility.

"Because you seem to have some reservations about an eye for an eye justice. You may wish to stay here and guard the house," Mr Hunter shrugged.

"Peace, gentlemen, this is not the time," Edward warned his cousin and his school friend.

"But you do bring up a good point, Hunter, someone should stay here at the house," Thomas replied.

"Arwyn, Edryd and Derwyn will be here, they will be quite enough," Gordon assured Thomas. The sound of movement upstairs heralded the emergence of the doctor from Miss DeVille's bedside.

"Very well, doctor, I hope that you are coming too. We do not know what condition the two women will be in and we may need your talents," Mr Hunter said as he heaved himself out of one of the two chairs that sat beside the fireplace.

"Of course, but it may be best if you were to remain

behind here. You have not had nearly enough rest," Jack Hales replied sternly as he descended the staircase.

"If I do not go, then no one will go," Mr Hunter said as he tried to stretch under the low ceiling.

"I am sure that we will find our way without you," Mr Brown assured the groundskeeper.

"No, we won't. Not even then men that have lived here for years found that place when sent to look for Millie and Grace. Hunter is the only one who has been there. He goes or no one does," Gordon countered forcefully.

"Well then, if you gentlemen or quite finished, the Baker boys will be nearly done by now," Lady Sarah announced as she and Sylvia appeared. Both were now dressed in jodhpurs and white shirts that were covered by men's riding coats that had been tailored to fit the female form.

Mr Hunter and Mr Brown both grinned at her appearance as she walked down the stairs.

"Discretion, gentleman, is the better part of valour," Edward hissed to his cousin and school friend when he noticed their expressions and the others all prepared to leave.

"Don't forget your cloaks," Thomas said as he passed the two men.

"How is Annie, doctor?" Lady Sarah asked in a quiet tone as the men bustled around them.

"Annie? Oh, Miss DeVille, she is not well. Her temperature has already begun to rise but I fear that is partially hysteria over being poisoned. Resting and staying calm are her best options until I can find out more about what exactly this poison is. Anything I could prescribe her could make the poison act faster or even become more deadly and I do not wish to put any in this house through another loss," the doctor replied.

"Thank you, we should hopefully have answers soon," Lady Sarah said with a mechanical smile.

By the time the group had gathered their cloaks, the Baker boys had the horses waiting in the farmyard for their riders. Mr Hunter was glad to be able to climb back into the saddle of his own horse.

Harald was a comfortable mount that did not have the same fire and spirit as Black Guy. The brigadier had originally bought Harald for his own use, but after seeing how easy the companionship was between Lady Sarah and

Mr Hunter, he had gifted the horse to his son.

Harald had a mild nature, he was an easy-going gelding that was fairly unshakeable but you importantly, he was comfortable to ride. Not too round with an easy reaching stride that made it feel as though he was barely moving. The perfect horse for a tired and stiff man to ride at a time like this.

Black Guy, by comparison, was far more suited to Lady Sarah's temperament. He was a stallion, high-strung with a wild streak that was masked by his fine appearance. He stepped high and purposively which could often be jarring for an inexperienced horseman.

He was far more sensitive to his rider's mood than any horse that Mr Hunter had ever come across, and he seemed to be so in tune with Lady Sarah that it was although the pair had been destined to be partners.

Harald was equally pleased to have his master back in the saddle, and Black Guy was happy to have his mistress take the reins. The horses that had drawn the carriages had been saddled for the others and two of the farm ponies had been saddled for the Baker boys to ride.

Neither boy was prepared to stay behind whilst the

others rode off to rescue Grace and Millie.

Pattinson was equally eager to be off. He did not know the purpose of the excursion, but he fed off the anxiety and tensions of those around him and barked and leapt around Black Guy as Lady Sarah swung herself into the saddle.

When everyone was mounted and ready to go, Mr Hunter rode out at the head of the party, the Baker boys bringing up the rear. Pattinson trotted along beside Harald at the front, his ears pricked and his eyes bright.

Chapter 19

Grace sat alone in her room after Mr Hunter had left. She didn't know what she was going to do when the two men woke up.

Mr Land and Mr Beets would know straight away that it had been her who had set Mr Hunter free. There was no way he could have escaped without help. She sat on the edge of her bed and thought would soon be light and if she was going to act, then she had to act now.

She took a few moments, to think about how her perspective had changed since seeing Mr Hunter in the house. It had been so long since she'd seen a friendly face. she'd lost all thought of escape and hope. But now, knowing everyone was so close, she couldn't help but think that there was a way out for her.

She steeled her resolve, stood and quietly crept across the floor to the door. She knew that Mr Hunter had seen Millie on the upper floors of the house. In all the months she had been held captive, she had never strayed beyond the area that the men had allowed her to roam.

Everything in her told her that she should stay where she was and wait, but she knew that she needed to find Millie so the two of them could attempt to escape.

~*~*~

The horses clattered through the forest. The path that Mr Hunter had carved on the trees was hard to see, even for him when moving at speed.

There was no denying, even for Mr Brown, that without Mr Hunter they would never have been able to find the trail.

The groundskeeper led them through the trees at a walk. The trees were too thick for them to travel any faster, and they were forced to ride in single file. It was apparent to all why the house had remained hidden for so long. If the forest had been less dense, it would have been far easier to discover the crumbling wreck, and it was ever more obvious to Lady Sarah, with every passing second, why they had chosen to hide away in such a place.

The kidnappers could not have asked for a more perfect place to hide. Had it not been for Mr Hunter getting lost, they would have never found their lair.

The riders were silent as they moved, each lost in their own thoughts. Each knew there could be only one course of action when they reached the house. The two men inside the kidnappers would have to be dealt with.

Gordon's path was clear to him. These men had robbed him of time with the one he loved. Therefore, he would have robbed them of more than that. Having his brother and father would make it harder for him. But he was no less resolved on the matter.

Lady Sarah could see the desperation in his eyes and knew what he was thinking.

As they reined their horses in at the edge of the clearing, she tried to convince the doctor to keep his son outside whilst the rest of them went in.

But there was nothing that anyone could do to stop Gordon from going into the house.

It stood looking completely innocent. The outline of it crumbling against the dark background of the still trees made it seem so unassuming. There was nothing about it to suggest that had hidden two desperate kidnappers and their victims for so long.

Nothing moved in the woods or in the house. The group sat and watched for a moment before they dismounted and tethered their horses to the trees.

Thomas elected to stay and guard them, as well as keeping a lookout just in case anybody approached the house that they were not expecting. After all, there had to be several people working with these men in order to pull off such an elaborate scheme.

There was also still the question of the children disappearing from the village that needed to be answered. It was something that had slipped the minds of many of their party with everything that had happened at the farm in the last few days. But it was something that Silvia was determined not to forget.

Before Gordon could get his hands on either of the men. She would find out what had happened to the children and if there was any hope of returning them home again.

Mr Hunter led the way to the house from the front. Lady Sarah was behind him. The doctor elected to stay at the rear and wait to be called inside should he be needed.

Alex tried the door, expecting it to be locked, but to his surprise, it opened easily.

Inside he could hear the voice of Mr Land calling out to them,

"Ah, finally. You've arrived. Come in, won't you, and take a seat."

Mr Hunter bridled at the tone of the man's voice. It was confident, clear and cocky. Something that no man in his position should be.

Lady Sarah placed her hand upon his arm to calm him. Alex leant back against the wall, allowing the young lady to step past him. She walked into the kitchen area with dignity and poise. Richard followed close behind at her shoulder.

The two made for an intimidating pair with the authority with which they entered the room.

By the fireplace, they could see Mr Beets and Mr Land both sitting in moth-eaten chairs that had long since passed any form of comfort.

Mr Beets had his fists clenched and resting on his knees. He looked like a cornered beast that was ready to fight its way free, but he was kept quiet for the moment by his compatriot.

Mr Land arose from his chair and with an open arm indicated that the pair should sit in the two empty seats that sat opposite theirs by the fire.

Mr Hunter, Gordon, Edward, Mr Brown, Stanley and Lee Baker all stepped into the room in turn behind Lady Sarah and moved to block the other doorways.

Lady Sarah strode across the floor. Every step seemed to be taken, with one goal in mind, reaching the two men that sat beside the fireplace without losing her composure.

Richard followed her at a similar pace as the others watched from around the room. There was a great deal of tension in the air.

Lady Sarah did not take her eyes off the two men. Her gaze was fixed on them as she approached, her face calm. She did her best to keep everything she was feeling in check. All her anger and frustration would have to wait until after she had finished questioning the two men.

She reached the two chairs and sat in the one opposite Mr Land. Richard opted to remain standing at her shoulder.

"I see you brought many bodyguards with you, my lady," Mr Land said, with a jovial tone.

"I brought friends, Lady Sara replied curtly. Now, if you would be so kind as to tell me where Grace and Millie are, we will collect them and be on our way," she said in a non-threatening voice, but the weight that carried with it told the two men that this was not a request but an order.

"My dear lady, we cannot simply hand over such valuable commodities such as these without at least some discussion of price," Mr Land said with a laugh.

"I do believe that you completely misunderstand the situation you are in, sir," Lady Sarah said, "If you do not tell us where the two ladies are, we will tear apart the whole of England, Scotland, Wales and all the corners of the Empire in search of them."

Mr Land flinched internally at the sound of her voice. It was all too familiar to the one that his employer used when she was dissatisfied with him.

Mr Beets squirmed slightly, doing his best to control his anger. If he launched himself at the lady, he did not know what would happen. The two men had not noticed the great Akita until now.

He came into the house at the back of the party with the doctor and tried to stay out of sight. He was a hunting dog. His instincts told him that his prey was within the walls, and therefore he used his mistress' friends as a distraction so that he could stalk his prey.

The two men were now very painfully aware that the dog had appeared on the other side of Lady Sarah to Richard. It sat by her leg looking completely placid. But with every twitch that Mr Beets made, the dog's ears pricked, and its eyes followed him with the slightest hint of the great teeth that were hidden behind the soft jaws.

"Well, I'm afraid that we are men of commerce and business milady. We do nothing without considering profit," Mr Land sneered, "Perhaps you would think of it as compensation for taking such good care of the two ladies."

"I think that you have taken more than just the two ladies in the name of commerce," Sylvia spat from behind them. Mr Land wheeled around in his chair.

Lady Sarah and Sylvia's eyes blazed with a fire that Mr Land had rarely seen in women before. His employer was a strong woman, but she had cold calculating eyes when she spoke to him and an authority that radiated from her.

Lady Sarah and Sylvia both had the same aura about them, but they were determined women who would stop at nothing to protect others and save them. This was very different from what he was used to.

"What is it that you think I have taken?" Mr Land asked.

"The children of Ashdown," Sylvia said quite simply.

Mr Beets leapt to his feet, causing Patterson to growl and do likewise. Lady Sarah placed her hand gently on Patterson's collar to keep him by her side.

"I would not do anything rash if I were you," Lady Sarah warned Mr Beets. He looked at Sylvia and the great hunting dog and slowly sat down again. His anger burned deep within his chest.

"I see we may have struck a nerve. Where are the children of Ashdown?" Lady Sarah asked calmly.

"Gone," Mr Beets said.

"What do you mean gone?" Sylvia demanded.

"There is a great deal of labour needed all around this great nation and the Empire. We are simply providing a low-cost source of labour in the form of these children. They were doing nothing in Ashdown. Their parents did not put them to work in the fields. The children were merely extra mouths to feed without offering anything in return. That is not the way this world works. One must work to survive. No matter how old one might be," Mr Land said.

From behind Lady Sarah, Mr Brown laughed.

"An empire built on blood. I see," he drawled, "It's no wonder that our founding fathers wished to leave for a better life overseas," he sighed.

"Come now sir, the world works in very simple, very specific ways. There is nothing to say that those over in the colonies do anything differently to us here, perhaps not using children. But I am sure you have slaves of your own. Gentlemen do not dirty their hands with labour, and you, sir, are quite clearly a gentleman. Tell me. Have you ever worked for a thing a day in your life? Or were you merely given money at birth and been taught how to wield it over others?" Mr Land asked acidly.

"I should think a man as educated as you seem to be we're not jumped to such conclusions about anyone in this room. Least of all our friend from America," Lady Sarah said in reply

"Ah. I feel I have struck a nerve with you as well, my lady. I doubt that you have ever had to work for anything," Mr Land sneered.

"Her Ladyship may not have worked for anything. But she has done a great deal of good in her lifetime. Even in the short time I have known her. More than can be said for someone like you," Sylvia spat in reply, her tongue clicking over every word purposefully to give each to give it more to give her speech more force,

"I have worked for everything in my life. I have been mistreated by men like you. I have been thrown out of society, cast aside, cast out, ostracised. And yet, Lady Sarah was quite happy to accept me into her household. She extended a hand in friendship. She does not expect anything from me that she would not do herself. You, sir, are a leech on society and have no place to judge a woman such as her."

Mr Beets cast a sideways glance at Mr Land and wondered what it was that he was going to do next. His friend was the brains of the operation. He was the one that thought their way out of situations. And for all intents and purposes, Mr Beets could see that he was going to fail.

The two women who were out talking him, and the men around the room would be more than a match for the two of them. Even if Mr Beets managed to bloody the noses of one or two of them, the dog would surely drag him down in moments and do more damage to him than he could ever do to anything there.

He felt the sting of defeat creeping up inside his stomach. He had to make a choice whether he would survive and escape, or whether he would stand by his friend to the bitter end.

To call him a friend was laughable. But he was the closest thing that Mr Beets had ever had to someone he could trust. But this was a cruel world. A world that forged men like Mr Beets that caused men and women to enslave others to do their dirty work. To force children to work in squalid conditions simply to earn a little money to help put food on the table.

"We took the children we didn't ask we just took we told the people that Ashdown that if they told anybody about it would come back and burn everything they had. They were happy to leave and lose the children in order to keep their farm. Fewer mouths for them to feed more money for them," Mr Beets replied.

"I don't think that any parent could ever be so callous as to cast out a child like that," Lady Sarah replied heartily.

"Then you, my lady, have never struggled for money. You have never struggled for anything. You don't know, the desperation that some people sink to. Not everybody in this world is good and kind. You'll learn that soon enough. There's a list of where all the children went in the drawer over there. I've seen him keeping him if you want to go find them. I'm sure, you can argue a good price for the children. The amount we sold them for is in there as well. I doubt the employers will let them go for any less than three times what they paid for them. But you're a woman of means. That shouldn't be a problem for you," Mr Beets said.

Richard crossed the floor and slowly opened the door and saw the list that Mr Beets was talking about. He picked it up and examined it. The handwriting was rough. The pen and the paper were both poor quality, but he could read enough to know where to begin. He nodded to Lady Sarah who smiled.

"Thank you, sir. Now for Grace and Millie as well," Lady Sarah said firmly.

"Even if we were willing to give you the list of the children, I'm afraid we cannot part with the two ladies," Mr Land said, "Well, we can perhaps part with one of them but not the other," he smiled maliciously.

"Why only one of them?" Lady Sarah asked.

"Well, only one of them is here now I'm afraid the other while she left some time ago," Mr Land said smugly.

"What do you mean she left some time ago? Which, which woman are you talking about?" Gordon demanded. Edward stood beside him and gripped the upper arm of the man to stop him from charging forwards.

"The mousy one, she's gone. The one who was looking after him when he came snooping the first time," Mr Beets said as he pointed at Mr Hunter.

"What do you mean gone?" Mr Hunter asked, "She would not leave here without Millie. She was not going to abandon her friend."

"She may not have intended to abandon her friend. But in the end, there was nothing she could do," Mr Land replied with a shrug.

"Where is she?" Mr Hunter growled.

" Well, that I'm afraid is something I can't tell you. I don't know," Mr Land replied and cast a sidelong at Mr Beets.

Mr Beets scowled at the man to his left.

"She's passed on," was all Mr Beat said.

The hand restraining Gordon could not hold on any longer as he lunged forward and grabbed at Mr Land's collar, forcing the chair over so that two men tumbled across the floor.

"Where is Millie?" he demanded.

Mr Land was silent but had a rather smug grin on his face. Out of some sense of misplaced loyalty, Mr Beets rose from his chair and launched at Gordon as he sat on top of Mr Land.

As he moved, Pattinson moved too. The dog was quicker and sank his great jaw around the outstretched arm of Mr Beets. Mr Beets howled in pain and tried to shake the dog off begging for mercy. All this did was make Pattinson bite down harder.

"We will search the house," Edward said and motioned for Mr Brown, Stanley and Lee Baker to follow him. Leaving Gordon, Richard, Mr Hunter, Doctor Jack Hales and Lady Sarah with Sylvia in the main room.

"Sylvia, go with them," Lady Sarah said, looking at her with a warning in her eyes.

"My lady, I don't think you should remain here either," Sylvia said.

"No. Probably not. But if I am here, then at least I can stop things from going too far afield," Lady Sarah replied.

"Doctor. I believe you'll be needed in a moment," Lady Sarah said as she went to release Mr Beets' arm from Pattinson.

Mr Hunter crossed the floor as Lady Sarah moved and took hold of Mr Beets from behind, his arm around his neck.

"Now if you move you'll only hurt yourself," Mr Hunter said, and Mr Beets had the good sense not to resist.

Pattinson released his arm at the slightest touch from Lady Sarah, and the doctor came to examine the wound.

Richard tried to hold Gordon and pull him back off Mr Land to prevent him from raining down blows on the man's face. But his attempts were in vain.

Gordon had tipped himself over the edge with the thought that Millie could be dead and gone as well as Grace.

There was no time for grief. There was too much they still had to do but the shock of Grace being gone was resonating within each of them.

None of them wanted to believe it just yet. After all, the two men could have been lying to make sure that they would leave without any sign of her.

Richard eventually managed to drag his brother free of Mr Land as he tired, but Mr Land's face was no longer as perfect as it had been before.

It was covered with bruises. And Lady Sarah was certain that a few teeth had been lost. The man was too badly beaten now to rise from the floor. And as soon as the doctor had finished with Mr Beets' arm, he went over to examine Mr Land.

Lady Sarah looked around the kitchen and found some old ropes so that Mr Beets could be tied up, and when he was Mr Hunter went to help Richard calm Gordon. Pattinson stood guard over Mr Beets.

"You need to calm yourself, Gordon. We don't know that either of them are dead just yet. Please take a breath,"

Mr Hunter urged.

The others made their way up the stairs. Sylvia did not go with the men but rather to Grace's room. She studied the room, and as far as she could tell, there was nothing missing from it.

Her hair brushes were sat on the table. Old ratty things but still have brushes that clearly were past the point of usefulness. The clothing that she had been allowed was hanging in the small cupboard and folded in the drawers. These few meagre possessions that she had been given whilst in captivity were all exactly what Sylvia thought they should be.

And yet Grace was gone.

She walked out of the room and back down the stairs slowly. The commotion that had been coming from the floor below had ceased.

Gordon sat in one of the two chairs opposite the two men responsible for kidnapping Grace and Millie. Richard and Mr Hunter were standing on either side of him each with a hand on each of his shoulders, keeping him in the chair.

Lady Sarah sat in the chair beside him watching the

doctor work. Mr Beets had an expression of defeat on his face. Pattinson, his eyes fixed firmly on the man, responded to any slight movement and Mr Beets knew that escape was now impossible for him.

"Mr Hunter, a moment if you please," Sylvia said, and Mr Hunter turned and came over to her at her beckoning.

"What can I do for you?" he asked with a slight edge to his voice.

"I need your assessment of the room. I need to know a few things and if anything is missing. You're the only one that has seen Grace after all this time. If there is anything that you notice in that room to suggest that she left of her own volition we need to know now," Sylvia said calmly and civilly.

Mr Hunter left nodded and followed Sylvia up to what they assumed was Grace's room. Mr Hunter looked around. There was a pair of shoes under the bed that Sylvia had not noticed before.

"Those are the shoes she was wearing yesterday. Mr Hunter said.

"I see," Sylvia replied, "That is all I needed to

know," she said sadly.

Mr Hunter watched as she walked back down the stairs, and followed quickly after her. The shift in her demeanour worried him. Sylvia crossed the floor and confronted Mr Beets with a cold look on her face.

"How many pairs of shoes did you give Grace?" she asked coldly.

"None," Mr Beets replied, "She had what she came with and that was it."

"I see," Sylvia said.

"What is it?" Mr Hunter asked with a frown from behind Sylvia.

"Grace had only one pair of shoes, you confirmed that the shoes under her bed were the ones that she was wearing yesterday. Mr Beets has told me that she only had one pair of shoes. She has not left under her own power. Unless she is hidden away in the house, I believe that she is buried somewhere in the woods," Sylvia sighed.

Mr Beets couldn't help but crack a slight smile at the thought process of Sylvia.

"Pattinson, we will need your help," Sylvia said firmly and the smile disappeared from Mr Beets' face.

"Wait until the others come down. Then we can go in groups and search," Lady Sarah said sadly. She didn't let the mask fall from her face. She kept all of her emotions pushed deep inside her heart for the moment. There would be time for grieving later. But for now, at least they still had a chance to find Millie alive.

Further up in the house, Lee and Stanley Baker were doing their best to search each room quickly. Edward and Mr Brown had found a locked door, one that needed to be forced open. The two men were doing their best to throw the door open whilst the two young boys searched the rooms.

Stanley and Lee ran as fast as they could from room to room, their feet pounding on the floorboards. Every so often they would run too fast and skid over a section of polished wood or trip over a loose rug, but their frantic searching turned up nothing.

Edward and Mr Brown were beginning to tire in their efforts to break down the door when the wood splintered and finally gave way. The two men practically fell through the doorway and collapsed into a pile on the floor.

The room beyond the door was dark and dusty. But it was by no means empty, as in the middle of the room and sat in the middle of the floor was Millie.

"We've found her!" Edward cried out, his voice only reaching as far as Stanley and Lee, who both rushed down to the kitchen to deliver the news.

They did not need to speak a word for Gordon to know, he simply read the two faces of the boys, pulled himself free of his brother's grasp and rushed off up the stairs.

"What is it?" Lady Sarah asked anxiously.

"We've found Millie, she's alive," Lee said with a grin.

"Doctor, I believe it would be best if you were to go upstairs with Lee and Stanley. We shall make our way outside with our friends. We have someone else to find," Lady Sarah said coldly as she felt a great sense of relief that at least Millie was alive.

"We're coming outside with you. There's nobody else in the house," Stanley snorted as he pointed the way up the stairs for the doctor.

Lady Sarah was about to dismiss the boys when she

felt Richard's hand on her shoulder. She glanced up at his face and he gently shook his head.

"Very well," she sighed and Richard and Mr Hunter took hold of their prisoners and pushed them out of the door ahead of the group.

Mr Brown and Edward had both returned the group to give Gordon and Millie some privacy and the doctor some space to do his work.

Pattinson trotted alongside Lady Sarah as she walked slowly out at the back of the group with Sylvia beside her. The men all charged ahead, keen to begin the search of the trees.

The trees looked the same in every direction as the group looked out for any signs of where Grace could have been taken.

Sylvia had fetched Grace's shoes so that Pattinson had something to find a scent from to track her. The hunting dog buried his nose in the shoes and then raised his head to the wind. He sniffed and began to walk in all different directions as he sniffed the ground.

The group was so fixated on what Pattinson was doing that they were not paying enough attention to what

Mr Land and Mr Beets were doing.

The next thing anyone knew, Thomas had cried out and the two men were running towards the edge of the trees.

"Quickly, we must stop them!" Mr Brown shouted.

"No, let them go, " Lady Sarah said, "We cannot waste any more time on those men. We have to find Grace and then I must set about finding these children," she clutched the list in her hand as she spoke and watched the two men disappear into the forest with a tinge of regret that the two men would not face justice.

Mr Land and Mr Beets did not look back as they ran. The ropes that had held them had been easy to break and it had only taken the smallest lapse in concentration by their captors to set them at liberty.

They did not hear the sound of the dog bearing down on them or of them being pursued. As they plunged into the trees, Mr Land risked a glance over his shoulder and saw they were not being chased.

He grinned to himself and slowed to a jog. Both he and Mr Beets had spent enough time walking these woods to know the routes in and out of the trees.

By the time the pair had reached the far side of the forest they had slowed to a walk and were sure that they would not be caught.

"You were right, dear brother, to think we should wait here," Derwyn's voice said with an element of smug satisfaction.

The two men looked around desperately as men seemed to appear from nowhere. Derwyn, Arwyn and a handful of men from the farm were with them.

"I assume this means that we are under arrest?" Mr Land asked coolly as he looked at the constable with a nervous eye.

"I wouldn't know, I am not here," Arwyn shrugged and turned away from the two men, "Put them with the pigs like Simon," he said in a low voice to his brother as he walked away from the group and through the trees to find his friends.

Chapter 20

They searched for almost two days in every corner of the trees for any sign of Grace's body but found none.

Derwyn and the farmhands had done their best to get any information out of Mr Land and Mr Beets as they could but it was to no avail. Both men feared the wrath of their employer far more than any threat that they could make.

By the time Lady Sarah and her companions arrived back at the farm with Millie, there was no sign of any of the men involved in the plot. Mr Brown had begun to make enquiries as to their whereabouts, but a quiet word from Thomas had stopped the questions.

There was no doubt in Lady Sarah's mind that the farmhands and the Evans family had handed out their own measure of justice, and after all they had endured, she could understand why they would rather do it themselves than allow any court or prison to hand out a suitable sentence.

She did not necessarily agree with their choice of action, nor could she say whether she would have done the same in their position or not. What she could say for certain was that the family and farmhands would all sleep soundly in their beds without any shred of guilt or doubt that they had done the right thing.

Millie was given a day or two resting at the farmhouse before the group decided it was time to leave Wales and return to Stickleback Hollow.

Those that could, spent every waking moment searching for Grace, but it was fast becoming clear to all of them that it was a wild goose chase. Edryd promised that he and his men would all keep searching after they had left, but Lady Sarah knew that they would never find her.

Miss DeVille had not died, but nor had she recovered. There was no way in which she could leave the farm and live. Derwyn had decided that he would not be returning to Stickleback Hollow, but remain with Miss DeVille and his mother to help nurse them both.

Doctor Hales was sure that Bronwyn would make a full recovery given time, but Miss DeVille's prognosis was not so bright. Edryd had hired a girl from the village to come and help around the house until Bronwyn was back on her feet, and with her, some semblance of normalcy would return to the farm.

The disappointment at not finding Grace had left Lady Sarah in something of a morose mood. She did not mope but she was more than a little out of sorts and not able to hold a conversation without drifting off partway through.

It was so unlike her that Mr Hunter elected to ride back to Stickleback Hollow in one of the carriages so that Lady Sarah could ride Black Guy home with Arwyn for company on Harald.

Early on the morning that had been designated as the date of their departure, Lady Sarah and Arwyn made ready to leave and said their goodbyes to their friends and to those that they would leave behind in Wales.

Pattinson was eager to join them on their ride home, but Mr Hunter made sure the dog stayed with him so that he could ride in the carriage.

Gordon and Millie travelled in the carriage with Mr Hunter and Pattinson. It was by far the largest and most comfortable carriage which was deemed best by the doctor, as he was certain that Millie would need a few weeks yet before she was completely physically recovered from her ordeal.

The doctor, the Baker Boys and Sylvia travelled in the smallest coach together, and Richard, Thomas, Edward and Mr Brown travelled together in the medium-sized carriage.

There was a little more room for the four men on the journey, but the trip was far less jovial than the trip out had been.

Mr Hunter closed his eyes and slept away most of the journey. The carriage called back at the same inn on the way home so that the horses could rest and the group could spend the night.

Sylvia and Millie shared a room but neither spoke a word to the other.

They bid goodbye to the Tatton Park party after they passed Chester, and Mr Hunter and Pattinson transferred to the carriage with Richard, so that Gordon and Millie could have some time alone for the last portion of the journey.

A great feast had been arranged by the brigadier to welcome Millie home. Lady Sarah and Arwyn had arrived back the day before the others which had given time for the welcoming party to be arranged, and for Arwyn to report to Captain Jonnes Smith that the case of the women's disappearance had been closed.

The feast was bittersweet, and as it came to an end it was punctuated by an announcement.

"Thank you for the warm welcome home. It is lovely to be back among friends, no matter how short-lived. But after all that has happened, and the danger that could still be out there, we have decided that we will be leaving Stickleback Hollow," Millie said timidly to the assembled party.

"Where do you plan to go?" the brigadier asked with a frown.

"We are going to go to America. Mr Brown's relatives are happy to welcome us to the New World, but we cannot stay here. We need a fresh start in a new place," Gordon explained.

"Well, son, I wish you and Millie well," the doctor said warmly, though the news was clearly breaking his heart.

The evening ended with a toast to the memory of Grace, after which Sylvia excused herself and retired to her room.

She sat in the dim light cast by a single candle and thanked God that she had been delivered home to Grangeback safely.

She was extremely sad about Grace, though she had never met the girl, she lived in her shadow and saw the regard that Lady Sarah held her in. It would take a long time before Lady Sarah would recover from yet another loss, but Sylvia was determined to do all she could to protect Lady Sarah from any further pain.

For now, they had the list of places the children of Ashdown had been sold to, and those children to free from the slavery they had been sold into. Saving those children would keep Lady Sarah moving forwards from Grace's death and help it to mean something.

No matter how small the difference might seem. An action for good will bring light and hope to even the darkest places, she thought to herself as she blew out the candle and went to get some rest.

Chapter 21

Mr Hunter and the brigadier retired to the study after the feast was finished. It had been a long journey for the groundskeeper and there was much he had to talk about with his father from the last few months that had seen the brigadier called away on a matter of Queen and Country.

"You do not need to tell me anything of what has transpired here in my absence. Cooky, Mrs Bosworth, Mr Clayton, Miss Beaumont and the Reverend Percy Butterfield have all informed me of all that happened. I am somewhat disappointed in what I have heard, but I know that sometimes it is harder to come back and face our mistakes than it is to stay and face them in the first place. Has she forgiven you?" the brigadier said as Mr Hunter closed the door to the study behind them and George fixed them both a drink.

"She has. She forgave me the moment she spoke to me when I returned. I did not expect that she would, but she did," Mr Hunter sighed.

"Then it is in your hands as to the future of your relationship. What do you make of Sylvia?" George asked as he sat down.

"She is somewhat cold. I saw you talking to her before the banquet, what did you say to her?" Mr Hunter asked.

"The day that you and my dear ward met is a day that I feel all criminals that cross your path will wish had never come to pass. As dear a girl as Grace was, she was not equal to the rigours that a life connected to a woman like Lady Sarah. You, on the other hand, are the perfect counterpart to her and I could think of a better person for the role. Protect her when I cannot and help her in ways no other can. No matter how long it is you do that for, you will always have a home here," the brigadier said warmly.

"I see, I thought you believed I was her equal and the perfect counterpart to her?" Mr Hunter frowned.

"Perhaps you are, but she needs an equal of her own sex to travel her path with for now. If she chooses to share her life with you, I will be the happiest father and guardian that has ever been. But Sylvia is loyal to Lady Sarah not out of anything other than friendship, and the purity of their friendship has a strength that cannot be denied and perhaps will outlast any form of romance in either of their lives. Don't fret too much, my boy. She will come around to you, I am sure," the brigadier grinned.

"I hope so," Mr Hunter shrugged helplessly.

"Did you speak to Mr Brown?" the brigadier asked with a wry smile on his face.

"About what?" Mr Hunter asked with a scowl.

"He has decided to stay in England for a while. He is purchasing Duffleton Hall so that he is not burdening his cousins at Tatton Park," the brigadier said with a slight grin.

"Did he speak to you about this?" Mr Hunter asked, glaring at his father.

"He did, and he also expressed his intentions to woo and marry Sarah," the brigadier replied.

"And what did you say to that?" Mr Hunter asked with an appalled look on his face.

"That she is in a time of grieving and needs to be allowed her space to do so. There will be no attempts to court her until she has come to terms with Grace's death," George said lightly.

"Good," Mr Hunter said with relief.

"The same applies to you, my dear son. She has had her heart hurt enough for now. Let her heal and she will make her own decision about her future and her own heart when she is ready. I do hope that it is you, but I will not force any decision upon her, and I will not allow anyone else to do so either," the brigadier warned, and the pair lapsed into silence as they drank.

Lady Sarah retired to her room quietly to be alone with her thoughts. She was happy for Millie and Gordon and understood the need for a fresh start in a new country. It had not been her choice to move to England from India, but now she would not change a thing for all the silver in China.

She also had another motive for going to her room alone. A letter had arrived for her during her time in Wales, and she had been unable to find a moment to sit and read it since her return.

It had come all the way from India and the paper had the familiar scent of spices that flooded her mind with memories of her youth.

The letter was from Captain Wilbraham Egerton and

was an unexpected, but welcome surprise. When she sat on the small chaise in her room she opened the letter with alacrity and began to read it with rising alarm.

My dearest friend,

I come to you from what I believe will be my end. I do not wish you to blame yourself for my fate, no matter what anyone may say, my death is nobody's fault, save for perhaps my own.

The wounds I sustained in the last skirmish we had at the border have robbed me of what little strength I have left. So please indulge a dying man with his last words.

I had hoped to return home to see the Grand Tournament one last time, but it was not to be. I wanted to be there to stand up beside you when you finally do decide you have found a man who is worthy of you.

Instead, I must be satisfied with the knowledge that you are perhaps the smartest woman I have ever met and that you will choose a partner for life that you can respect and honour, and who in turn will do the same for you.

If it is not Mr Hunter, I will be exceedingly surprised. But do not let my opinion influence you too much, even if it is the opinion of a dying man.

I am truly blessed to have been able to count you amongst my friends, and I know that you will have a long life filled with adventures, something I truly envy you for. You are a lady who cannot help but find excitement and danger no matter where you go, and it will ensure your life shall never be dull. But please, be careful.

It may surprise you to learn that I am in the house of one Lady de Mandeville as I write to you. She offered to provide me with a bed away from the ghastly hospitals, but even a clean bed has not been enough to save me.

I have not been mistreated, on the contrary, I have been treated as an honoured guest, and her companion here is a military man, so it has been wonderful to compare our experiences in the service.

I know that you have already lost so much, but do not count me as a loss in your life. I may be gone but I will never be lost to you. Whether in life or death, know that our friendship shall abide and I will see you again when the Lord calls you home.

Do not leave this world with any regrets. The ones I carry to my grave seem to be so trivial now, but I would not have you be the same as I.

The greatest honour of my life has been able to fight beside a lady so strong and so bright, and even able to boast that I have saved that same lady's life.

Be well dear heart. I would not have you grieve for we shall meet again, someday, just think of me as I was when we danced at Tatton Park, full of life, just in another place. Close at hand, just out of reach, but always your loyal and devoted servant.

Adieu sweet lady, live well.

Wilbraham

~*~*~

Love the book? Need to know what's next in Stickleback Hollow?

Her nemesis is finally in front of her, but is this mastermind really the villain she appears to be? Or is there another who has been pulling the strings the whole time?

257

Get _Lady de Mandeville in Stickleback Hollow_ now!

~*~*~

Looking for more than just books? You can get the latest releases from me, signed paperbacks and hardbacks, mugs, t-shirts, journals and much more from my Read Round the Clock Shopify store.

~*~*~

Love the Mysteries of Stickleback Hollow? Not caught up with the rest of the series, then jump back to _A Thief in Stickleback Hollow_, Book 1 in the Mysteries of Stickleback Hollow and see how it all began.

~*~*~

Want to help a reader out? Reviews are crucial when it comes to helping readers choose their next book and you can help them by leaving just a few sentences about this book as a review. It doesn't have to be anything fancy, just what you liked about the book and who you think might

259

like to read it. **Scan the QR Code below** or visit

https://mybook.to/SpringinStickleback.

If you don't have time to leave a review or don't feel confident writing one, recommending a book to your family, friends and co-workers can help them choose their next book, so feel free to spread the word.

Historical Note

The Red Lion or Red Lyon Inn was established as far back as 1737 in Dodleston. The only notable occurrence at this particular inn was that during the autumn of 1845 there was a battle of sorts between enraged English and Irish farm labourers. Though this had not happened yet in Lady Sarah's timeline. I chose this particular pub, not only because Dodleston was quite wonderfully positioned for the purposes of the journey to Wales, but still exists as a pub to this day.

Carlo Pozzo di Borgo was the Russian ambassador to the United Kingdom of Great Britain and Ireland from 1835 until 1839. A Corsican by birth, he was considered a traitor to his country because of his opposition to Napoleon Bonaparte. He fought at the Battle of Waterloo and was singled out in Wellington's post-battle dispatch. He was regarded as a true gentleman and his deeply held sense of duty and honour is something I have tried to capture in the brief snapshots we see of him in the book.

In my initial research of Captain Wilbraham Egerton, there were conflicting sources as to whether he was part of the Tatton Park Egertons or if he even existed. The evidence that I found that did point not only to his existence but that he was part of the Egerton family, also said he died in India at the time this book is set. Because I chose to include him using this source material, I could not ignore his death. In the book, his injuries played some part in his death, but the cause of his death in real life is unknown to me. However, it seemed fitting that he would pen such a letter to Lady Sarah upon his death bed, especially after all she has had to endure until now.

Children were expected to work in Victorian Britain. Though children had worked for hundreds of years prior to the Victorian Era, the arrival of the industrial age meant that the need for cheap labour was greater than ever. Long work hours and terrible conditions were the norm for children as young as four and five years old. The poverty of many families during this time was one of the major reasons that so many children entered the workforce, as the additional income was necessary to help feed the family as a whole.

Children worked in a number of different sectors from farms to factories, servants in houses or even down in mines. There were a number of dangerous jobs that children were well suited to because of their small size, but it also meant that a lot of children often died due to the hazardous nature of their employment. Children who were chimney sweeps would get trapped in the chimneys they were sent up to clean and often suffocated in the small spaces.

In 1833 the Factory Act was introduced which prohibited the employment of children under the age of nine years old in factories. It also limited the number of hours children between the ages of 9 and 13 could work to no more than 48 hours. Many changes to the Factory Act and the Mining Act took place over the following 150 years. In 1875, chimney sweeps had to be licensed and licenses were not issued to sweeps who used climbing boys (the ones who would get stuck in the chimneys and die). In 1878 the employment of children under 10 was banned and regulations were introduced to monitor safety, ventilation and meals. In 1880 the Education Act made it compulsory for every child in the UK aged between 5 and 10 would be given an education in schools, but for free. Assisted Education wasn't provided until 1891. In 1918, the school leaving age was raised to 14, then in 1944 it was raised to 15, and in 1973 it was raised to 16. In 2008, children who started secondary education in September 2008 are now required to stay in compulsory education until they are 17 years old.

Slavery as a concept in the British Empire was not something new in the Victorian Era. It has existed in Britain since the Roman occupation of Britain in 43AD. During the 11th Century and the Norman Conquest of England, a merger began between slavery into serfdom. Though it was still unfree servitude, it was not quite the same concept as slavery. This continued until the 16th Century and the establishment of the Atlantic Slave Trade. Slavery was never legalised in England, and in the 1772 Somerset Case, Lord Mansfield ruled that as slavery was not recognised by English law, a slave named James Somerset, a slave who had been brought to England and subsequently escaped, could not be sent back to Jamaica to be sold as a slave again, and was sent free.

Despite its lack of legal standing, slavery still existed and in the 18th and 19th Century an abolitionist movement grew and, thanks to the efforts of William Wilberforce, led to the Slave Trade Act 1807' that abolished the Slave Trade in the British Empire but it wasn't until the Slavery Abolition Act 1833 that slavery was abolished within the Empire.

That did not mean that slavery disappeared from the Empire, it still existed in its illegal forms, and it even persists in the world today in the form of human trafficking, which is a worldwide problem. The 1811 Slave Trade Felony Act 1811, made the overseas trade slave trade a felony throughout the British Empire. The British Empire established a West African Squadron that was sent to suppress the Atlantic slave trade by patrolling the coast of West Africa. Though it made great strides in suppressing the Atlantic Slave Trade it did not stop entirely.

Between 1808 and 1860 the West African Squadron captured 1,600 slave ships and freed 150,000 African slaves. They were resettled in Jamaica and the Bahamas. Britain also used its power at the time to coerce other countries to agree to treaties that put an end to their own slave trade and allowed the Royal Navy to also seize their slave ships.

For the poor children of Ashdown, they served as merely an illustration of despite much being done to legally protect the rights of children and to abolish slavery, there were individuals who valued money over human life and would indulge in the illegal slave trade and child labour for their own greed and selfish gains.

The history of policing in the UK is an interesting read and stretches back to 1750 when two magistrates, Henry and John Fielding (brothers) of the Bow Street Magistrate court created a paid constabulary to help combat the crime in London. They were known as the Bow Street Runners. But it was not something that proved to be a popular idea and other cities and countries refused to do the same until the late 18th century. In 1798 the Thames River Police were formed and are recognised as the first regular professional police force in London. Dublin had, however, had a police force since 1786 when a professional uniformed and armed police force in Dublin was created to help support British rule in Ireland that was facing serious challenges and would continue to face with the approaching potato famine. It was reformed in 1795 and then again in 1808 and by 1812, when Robert Peel, the founder of modern policing, was appointed as the chief secretary for Ireland, Dublin was relatively crime-free.

The UK police are often referred to as Bobbies, Bobby's men or Robert's men, a nod to Robert Peel. In Wales, policing began in 1841 with the creation of forces in Glamorgan, Cardiff Swansea and Merthyr Tydfil which would eventually become the South Wales Constabulary in 1969. But there were areas where there was no official police force, so for the sake of law and order, the closest police force for our friends in Wales would be the Cheshire Police in the story (even though in reality I have moved the founding of the Cheshire Police to a few decades earlier than it was actually established).

At the start of Queen Victoria's reign, more than half of the population of Great Britain worked in the countryside. Landowners often had tenant farmers who in turn had labourers. The Evans family are landowners in our own tale who choose to farm it themselves as their family has always done so. This means that their labourers live in relative luxury compared to the other labourers of the time. The Brigadier as a landowner in Stickleback Hollow would have many tenant farmers who would work his land and they would, in turn, have farm labourers. A significant income would have come to the landowners from their farm tenants.

For farm labourers, they often lived in extremely cramped and basic conditions where they were given only a small plot of land to grow vegetables for themselves and a kept a pig to provide themselves with meat. Corn gleanings were collected after the corn harvest was taken and they were used to make flour and bread for their family. They would also make their own cider, ale and wine from fruits. Which is why the English have such things as Dandelion and

Burdock and Elderberry Wine.

Common lodging-houses were a cheap form of accommodation in the Victorian era where people lived together in communal rooms with shared common areas. These were found across the UK and the lower rent ones were more like flophouses than the bunk style house that the Evans maintain on their farm. In London, common lodging-houses became something of a scandal as they were often frequented by criminals and prostitutes which led to them being regulated under the Common Lodging Houses Acts 1851 and 1853.

However, these regulations did more to hurt the poor innocent occupants of the houses. They had to vacate the premises between 10am and late afternoon, which meant the poor and sick residents had to walk the streets when they were not allowed in their lodging, no matter what the weather was. It wasn't until 1894 that the regulation made a difference to the conditions in the housing. Walls had to be whitewashed with lime twice a year, and mixed-sex accommodation was abolished, so the brothels that operated out of them could no longer function. Beds with frames and proper bedding had to be provided; prior to this occupants were given mattresses on the floor or worse.

About the Author

I was born in Macclesfield, Cheshire, UK, and raised in the nearby town of Wilmslow. From an early age, I discovered I had a flair and passion for writing.

I began writing at the age of 7 and was first published in 2010. I currently live with my partner, Matt, and our two cats in Christchurch, New Zealand.

As an avid horsewoman and gamer, I also have a passion for singing, dancing, the theatre, and my garden.

Facebook: https://www.facebook.com/AuthorC.S.Woolley

Instagram: https://www.instagram.com/thecswoolley

Website: http://.mightierthanthesworduk.com

Acknowledgements

Writing can be an extremely lonely profession at times, but thankfully I never have to go through any of the pressures alone. My wonderful Matthew has been a source of constant support to me during all of my writing endeavours since we first met. I couldn't ask for a more fitting partner to share my life or love with.

Writing is not something I stumbled into either, my mother, Helen, took me, and my sisters, to the library every weekend when we were young to get different books, and I always maxed out the number of books I could get. Not only did she encourage me to read, but to write as well. To say I have been writing stories and poetry since I was 7 is not an exaggeration and the development of my writing career is due in no small part to her.

My mother-in-law, Lesley, has also been a source of

unflinching and unwavering support, something I could not do without.

To Laura and Sam, who have read and offered opinions, death threats and encouragement on my early drafts, you are true treasures. Amy, you too are worth your weight and more in gold for all your love and support.

It may seem that writers only function alone, but I am blessed to be part of an amazing community of authors whom I know who have helped push me to even greater heights and success. So to Quinn Ward, Donna Higton, Scarlett Braden Moss, Bryan Cohen, Chez Churton, Robert Scanlon, Jen Lassalle, Brittany Weese, Phoebe Ravencroft, and Marcel Liemant, my dear friends, thank you.

And finally, to you, dear reader, without you there would be no books, no series, no career. I want to thank you for all the time that you spend reading my work, reviewing it, and sharing it with your friends and family. Without you, there would be nothing. Thank you from the bottom of my heart.

Until we meet again in my next book, thank you and adieu.